UNDER MOONLIT ASHES

WRITTEN BY;
T.A. THORNWELL

PUBLISHED BY:
ASHEN VEIL PUBLISHING

CONTENTS

TRIGGER WARNINGS

For Under Moonlit Ashes

This novel is a dark fantasy romance intended for mature audiences (18+). It contains explicit content, emotionally intense subject matter, and disturbing themes that may be triggering for some readers.

Please proceed with caution.

- **Graphic Violence & Gore** – Includes visceral battlefield scenes, executions, torture, bloodshed, and depictions of death in vivid detail.

- **Obsession & Possessiveness** – Features unhealthy, all-consuming romantic fixation, emotional volatility, and toxic attachment.

- **Forced Cannibalism** – A disturbing scene involving coerced consumption of human flesh.

- **Non-Consensual Sexual Assault (Attempted)** – Includes a scene where a character is physically restrained and assaulted against her will.

- **Betrayal & Deception** – Central to the narrative are themes of manipulation, lies, shifting loyalties, and personal betrayals.

- **Dark Psychological Themes** – Explores madness, grief, moral collapse, emotional abuse, and identity trauma.

- **Power Imbalance & Domination** – Depictions of emotional coercion, manipulation, and relationships marked by significant imbalances of control.

- **Religious & Occult Symbolism** – Involves witchcraft, ancient gods, blood rituals, and spiritual corruption.

- **Supernatural Elements** – Includes ghostly apparitions, divine punishment, prophetic visions, and life-after-death experiences.

- **Death & Loss** – Major character deaths, prolonged

grief, suicide, and psychological trauma surrounding loss are central themes.

- **Corruption & Moral Decay** – Institutional rot, kingdom-wide corruption, and characters sacrificing morality for survival.

- **Fire & Burning Imagery** – Fire is used symbolically and literally; depictions include self-immolation, burning bodies, and scorched landscapes.

- **Parental Death & Childhood Trauma** – Includes violent death of parents and how the resulting trauma shapes characters long-term.

- **Psychological & Emotional Manipulation** – Core to many character arcs, including gaslighting, guilt-tripping, and emotional blackmail.

- **Explicit Sexual Content & Dark Romance (18+)** – Contains intense, graphic intimacy with dominant/submissive undertones, emotional obsession, and morally grey relationships.

- **Knife Play** - Contains scenes involving consensual knife play, sharp blades, controlled cuts, and physical power dynamics. Reader discretion is advised, especially for those sensitive to themes of pain, control, or weapon-based intimacy.

- **Blood Play** - This narrative features intense depictions of blood play, including ritualistic bleeding, blood magic, and erotic use of blood. These scenes are graphic and may be disturbing to some readers.

This is not a love story. This is obsession, betrayal, and fire. These are the ashes left behind.

TROPES
For Under Moonlit Ashes

Romantic & Emotional Tropes

- **Enemies to Lovers**: A forbidden romance between leaders of rival kingdoms.

- **Forbidden Love**: Their relationship defies kingdoms, duty, morality, and ends in tragedy.

- **Obsessive Love**: Possessive, all-consuming, and emotionally volatile.

- **Arranged Marriage**: Two Kingdoms with heirs meant to be married to unite the kingdoms.

- **Dark Romance**: Features morally grey characters, intense emotional stakes, and twisted intimacy.

- **Tragic Romance**: The lovers are doomed by fate, betrayal, and sacrifice.

- **Love Triangle (With Power Dynamics)**: A triangle of control, lust, and manipulation.

- **Love After Death**: Offers a final bittersweet intimacy.

- **Secret Child**: hides the child to protect her legacy.

Dark & Psychological Tropes

- **Morally Grey/Black Characters**: No true heroes. Everyone has blood on their hands.

- **Female Rage**: MFC gets pushed into a fit of rage.

- **Villain Love Interest**: Both antagonist and lover; ruthless, haunted, and mesmerizing.

- **Manipulative Mentor**: Orchestrates the fate of kingdoms from the shadows, playing everyone like pawns.

- **Fate vs. Free Will**: The story questions whether destiny is fixed or if it can be defied.

- **Trauma-Driven Character Arcs**: Each major character is shaped by deep psychological wounds.

- **Gaslighting & Emotional Manipulation**: Prominent in romantic and political dynamics alike.

- **Power Imbalance in Relationships**: Love is weaponized. Power is constantly shifting.

Fantasy & Political Tropes

- **Warring Kingdoms**: Eldoria vs. Morvath: swords clash, secrets burn, and empires fall.

- **Revenge Plot**: Motives for vengeance drive multiple arcs.

- **The Chosen One (Subverted)**: Destined for power, but it comes at a soul-shattering cost.

- **Secret Heir**: Hidden to protect her bloodline, with a future awaiting in shadows.

- **The Puppet Master**: Manipulates events across generations with precision and malice.

- **Royal Intrigue & Betrayal**: Court politics, power grabs, arranged marriage plots, and deadly deception.

- **Magical Forest**: Forest serves as a place of magic, danger, and fate-weaving.

Symbolic & Thematic Tropes

- **Fire as Metaphor**: Fire represents destruction, passion, rebirth, and fate throughout the book.

- **Death as Transformation**: Death marks beginnings, not just endings.

- **Ghostly Visitation**: Spirit returns, allowing for final closure (and temptation).

- **Sacrificial Love:** Both pay the price for their forbidden love.

- **There Is Always a Reckoning**: The past haunts the future. Fate collects what it is owed.

Hard-Hitting Tropes (Adult Themes)

- **Tortured Antihero**: Violent, scarred, seductive, and still capable of love.

- **Heroine Breakdown**: Emotional rock bottom in devastating, visceral ways.

- **Seduction as Strategy**: Characters use sex, love, and affection as weapons.

- **Non-Consensual Threats**: Includes scenes of attempted sexual assault and physical restraint.

- **Blood Magic / Soul-Binding**: Magic is dark, divine, and deeply personal.

- **Ghost Romance / Post-Mortem Longing**: Love lingers after death, and it hurts.

- **Deal with the Devil (or Witch)**: Character is tempted with an unholy deal.

Legacy Tropes

- **Hidden Legacy**: The daughter of fire and shadow is the secret future of two kingdoms.

- **Raised in Disguise**: Grows up unaware of her lineage, watched from the shadows.

- **Heir of Two Worlds**: She will one day inherit the consequences of both love and war.

ACKNOWLEDGEMENT

Special thank you to my Beta Readers

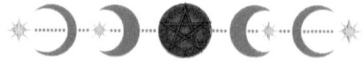

Rebecca Valderrama	Bethanys_bookshelf92
@saltynlm75	DarkandReckless
@k0rtnie	Militarywifea
AngieSue16	Marissa Bartley
Kristinaj13	Katherine Andy
@bookishmandi	@katlynjohnson03
Crescent.moon.alpha	Myranda_bookshelf
Keeks86__	@cheeto
Megan	Stephstory5150
@jacqueline_xo21	Cassie Tiner

I appreciate all the feedback that was given during the beta reading of this book. I have implemented quite a few of the ideas that were shared from the feedback. Just know, that without my beta readers, certain things in this book would simply not be there. I am eternally grateful and would like to see you guys on the next one!

Extra Special Thank you to my editor on this project

Senior Editor : C.A. Tiner

C.A. Tiner worked tirelessly on this book, read through it at least 100 times, countless hours to make sure everything was up to par. Bless her heart and soul. Without her, this book would simply not be possible. So, Thank you Cassie, from the bottom of my heart. Your hard work does not go unnoticed.

THORNWELL'S
NOTE TO THE READER

Hey. Before you dive in, I need you to understand something.

This is not your grandmother's love story. This is not light-hearted. This is not sweet. This book will not hold your hand or kiss your forehead and tell you everything's going to be okay.

This story goes to dark places...*deep* ones. It deals with obsession, grief, manipulation, death, power, and pain. If you find yourself needing a break...*take it*. Protect your peace. Protect your heart. Your mental health matters more than my fiction.

Now, if you're here hoping for comfort, sunshine, and neatly wrapped happy endings?

Close the book. Walk away. This is not that story. But...If you're the kind of soul who aches for tragedy...If you crave the burn that scorches, the love that bleeds, and the endings that ruin you? If you're a masochist who's in it *for the pain*?

Then do as you are told and turn the fucking page.

That's my Good Girl.

UNDER MOONLIT ASHES

SOUNDTRACK

This book has it's own Spotify soundtrack for you to listen to as you are reading.

1. Seven Devils – Florence + The Machine

2. Saturn – Sleeping At Last

3. Way down We Go – KALEO

4. Wicked Game (Cover) – Violet Orlandi

5. Arsonist's Lullabye – Hozier

6. Love is a Bitch – Two Feet

7. Dark Side – Bishop Briggs

8. Take Me to Church – Hozier

9. The Night We Met – Lord Huron

10. Young And Beautiful – Lana Del Ray

11. Skin – Rag' n' Bone Man

12. My Mother Told Me – Alina Gingertail

13. Echo – Jason Walker

14. I See Red – Everybody Loves an Outlaw

15. Glory and Gore – Lorde

16. Bury a Friend – Billie Eilish

17. The Devil Within – Digital Daggers

18. Angel of Small Death and the Codeine Scene – Hozier

19. In The End (Mellen Gi Remix) – Tomme Profitt, Gleurine, Mellen Gi

20. Tears of Gold – Faouzia

21. Run – Snow Patrol

22. Hurt – Johnny Cash

23. Nothing Else Matters – Metallica

24. My Blood – Ellie Goulding

25. Creep (Acoustic) – Radiohead

26. The Hanging Tree – James Newton Howard, Jennifer Lawrence

27. I'll Never Love Again (Film Version) – Lady Gaga, Bradley Cooper

28. A Thousand Years – Christinia Perri

29. My Immortal – Evanescence

PROLOGUE

ELYSANDRA

The night bled.

Not in a way that mortals notice, no crimson tides spilling from wounds in the sky, no shrieks on the wind. No, the forest bled quietly. The kind of bleeding that seeps into your bones and makes your teeth ache. A slow, ancient pulse, steady as a war drum muffled beneath a coffin lid.

The moon hung overhead, gaunt and pale, obscured by strips of withered cloud like the torn gauze of a grieving widow. She watched, reluctantly, through the gaps. Afraid. Wise.

Even the stars kept their distance. Cowards.

The Eldorian Forest stretched around me, old and hungry. Branches gnarled like arthritic fingers; trunks carved with the scars of forgotten rituals and failed resurrections. Roots shifted when you weren't looking. Some trees moved. Others listened. The air smelled of rot and sage, copper and cold earth. Something primal. Something divine.

Perfect.

They will tell you stories about me. Lies, mostly.

Some say I bathe in the blood of kings. Others whisper that I sold my soul for a crown I never wore. A forest witch. A temptress. A traitor to every throne. All of that is true, but none of it even touches the surface.

Look closely.

My eyes? Sharp as shattered obsidian. Green, like moss fed by centuries of rot and rain, hiding secrets under layers of ancient frost. They have seen the rise of empires, and the exact moment each one begins to rot from within. I don't blink at death. I study it. Improve it.

My hair is red...not the soft, romantic kind, but the hue of fresh blood spilled on snow. Long. Wild. Braided when I feel like pretending to be civilized but mostly left to cascade down my back like the flame I keep buried under my skin. It's been set on fire more than once. I always win.

I wear what suits the night. Leather, velvet, bone. Symbols carved into the seams... runes from a forgotten tongue. My corset laces tight enough to stop a man's breath, not mine. My boots are silent when I move. You'll never hear me coming, only feel the chill in the air a moment too late.

I walk like the forest follows me. Because it does.

My voice? Soft, until it isn't. I speak in riddles, in prophecies, in promises I intend to keep whether they ruin you or not. Every word I say is a thread in the tapestry of fate... and I never drop a stitch.

I am Elysandra; Witch of the Eldorian Forest, Weaver of fate, Harbinger of what is yet to come, cursed to walk among this realm for all eternity. Nine Centuries so far....

If you've come here for a fairy tale... you're in the wrong fucking forest.

I stood in the center of an ancient glade, where the ground remembered blood and the stones remembered names long buried beneath moss. The soil here was soft, but not from rain. Too much has been spilled in this place: sacrifices, secrets, souls. All of it still clung to the air like smoke clings to hair.

The ritual ring was almost finished. Nine layers, each more intricate than the last, traced in bone dust and ash from a flame that never burned out. Sigils curled and spiraled, scrawled in languages whose alphabets had been lost to time. The kind of words that would kill a priest if he dared to whisper them. A lullaby for the gods that stopped listening.

I dragged my finger through the final arc of the outermost circle, humming softly, a tune so old even I couldn't remember where it came from. Probably one of the civilizations I helped destroy.

"Seriously though," a voice wheezed behind me, "are we doing the dramatic spooky bitch thing all night or what? 'Cause I'm outta snacks and I swear this bone might've been a dog. Or a noble. Hard to tell. Taste-wise, I mean."

I didn't look up.

"I told you not to speak until the glyphs were sealed."

"And I told you not to name me after a chewing sound, but here we are."

A snap of twigs. A thud. Something wet sloshed.

Then came the waddling.

Nibbles, my chaos demon, my shame, my mistake, emerged from the gloom like sin itself had tripped over a root and landed face-first in sarcasm. He was a stunted horror; a foul little creature shaped vaguely like a raccoon but spliced with something far more infernal. His limbs were slightly too long. His fur was coarse and patchy, bristling like it was constantly annoyed to be on his body. His teeth gleamed with decay and mischief. His tail twitched erratically behind him, like it couldn't decide which plane of existence to be in.

That was Nibbles.

He stumbled into the edge of the ritual circle, chewing on what looked like a femur, eyes glinting with unholy glee. He wore a satchel made from stitched-together squirrel pelts. It had seen better centuries.

"Check it," he grunted. "Found a baby skull in that ditch you told me not to dig in. Still had teeth! I call dibs."

I sighed. "That was a sacred burial site."

"Sacred schmacred. It's just really well-organized garbage."

"You are a plague in a raccoon's body."

"You say that like it's a bad thing."

He plopped down next to the circle, the bone in his mouth making an audible *crack* as he bit through it like candy. Then he gagged.

"Blegh. That one had filling. Ugh. I think I chipped a tooth."

I said nothing. I'd learned not to encourage him. He thrived on attention like mold thrived on damp wood.

The dagger in my hand pulsed, a smooth obsidian blade older than the kingdoms rotting on either side of this forest. It fed on memory, and it was starving.

I pressed it to my palm and pulled. Blood spilled, thick and dark, smelling of yew and nightshade and distant thunder. It hissed as it touched the runes, each drop lighting the circle in a deep crimson glow. The air crackled. The ground trembled. The trees leaned in.

Power unfurled like wings.

I closed my eyes.

The weave shimmered behind my eyelids. I could see it now, the threads. Filaments of reality, winding like veins through the world, crisscrossing, tangling, snapping. Each thread a life. A choice. A consequence. I saw the girl again. Her silhouette outlined in firelight, crownless and defiant. I saw the man who followed her into madness, sword in hand, heart bared. I saw a kingdom bleeding beneath a sky that would not weep for it.

A future unwritten, because I hadn't written it yet.

Not quite.

I reached out, fingers ghosting over the strands of destiny.

"Uh, hey," Nibbles whispered far too loudly, "so... serious question: if you pull one of those and it unravels a nation, do I still get my Tuesday belly rub?"

"No."

"Not even a cursed tickle?"

"You don't *have* a belly."

"I *could*. Spiritually."

"Spirits want nothing to do with you."

"Oh, come on, Elysandra. Just admit it. You love me. In that 'I'd turn you into a toad if it were socially acceptable' kind of way."

I opened my eyes slowly and stared at him. His nose was now buried in a sack of stolen mushrooms that may or may not have been enchanted. He sneezed. The forest glowed blue for a moment.

He blinked. "...Oops."

I resumed the ritual before I had to burn the entire glade down.

The final glyph sizzled and died, consumed by its own power. The blood vanished into the dirt. The weave trembled.

The future was locked.

I wiped my hand on the inside of my cloak; the fabric already stained from dozens of spells cast in secret. My gaze drifted upward, to that coward of a moon, still hiding behind the clouds.

"Run," I whispered to it. "They're going to blame you when the fire consumes."

Nibbles climbed up a rock, striking a pose with his bone-sword held aloft.

"What fire?"

"The one I just lit," I murmured, too softly for him to hear.

Because I knew how this ends. Not from prophecy. Not from hope. From design.

I am the Fate-Weaver. I do not wait for the world to spin.

I shape it.

And when the final thread is cut, they will call it destiny.

But we'll both know it was me.

CHAPTER 1
THE IRON CAGE OF GRACE

SERAPHINA

T hey say the dawn breaks gently over Eldoria.

They're wrong.

It crashes like a blade unsheathed, slicing through the veil of sleep with its cold, unrelenting truth: another day in the castle, another performance. Another round of duty, of sacrifice, of silence, where I long to scream.

I am already sitting upright before the bells chime from the western tower. I don't sleep deeply. Not anymore. Not since the Queen died and the world demanded that I grow into her shadow before my body had even finished growing into itself.

The air in my chambers is crisp, touched by the bite of morning. A window is cracked open, just enough to let in the breeze from the mountains. It smells of pine and frost... freedom, in another life.

A soft knock sounds at the door. Once. Twice.

Then she enters.

Bethany.

She moves with the same rhythm every morning: silent, precise, as if her body is in perfect sync with mine. Her blonde hair is already neatly braided, wrapped around her head like a crown of woven gold. Her eyes... sharp and intelligent, sea-glass blue, find mine instantly.

She smiles. Not a forced one. A real one. The only real one I see.

"You're up," she says, though she already knew I would be.

"Did you expect me to sleep in and scandalize the court?" I ask.

Bethany smirks as she walks to the foot of the bed, unfolding my dressing gown. "Gods forbid the Lady Seraphina sleep past dawn. They'd call for your execution by breakfast."

"They already are," I mutter under my breath, slipping out from under the covers.

The stone floor is freezing beneath my bare feet. Bethany notices. She always does. She slides a pair of soft slippers near me with her toe before I even shiver. There's comfort in the way she anticipates my every need... not as a servant... but as someone who's seen every crack in my armor and never tried to patch them up.

She is my handmaiden. My lady-in-waiting. My shield. My keeper.

But above all, she is my only friend.

She helps me dress, tightening the corset laces with skilled fingers, never pulling too tight, always stopping just before I run out of breath. We don't speak much during the ritual. Words aren't necessary. She knows what's next. So, do I.

Bethany clears her throat and unrolls the parchment she brought with her.

"Today, you are expected at the council chamber by the second bell. Lord Malric has summoned the royal advisors to discuss grain shortages in the northern provinces. After that, weaponry drills with Captain Rhord. A midday inspection of the orphanage, followed by a diplomatic luncheon with the visiting noblewomen of Virel. After lunch, history lecture with the scribes in the East Wing. Tea with Lady Vessa. Choir rehearsal in the chapel..."

"I'm not even allowed to be tone-deaf in peace, am I?" I interrupt, rubbing sleep from my eyes.

Bethany grins. "You're not allowed to be anything but perfect."

I sigh. "Anything else?"

"A walk through the gardens, publicly, of course. And then a ceremonial offering at the Hall of Ancients. That one is non-negotiable. They're preparing a memorial for the Queen."

The Queen... my mother.

I freeze for a moment. A pause that tastes like ashes.

I nod once, curtly, and press on. There is no time to grieve. There hasn't been in months.

Bethany folds the parchment with a softness that doesn't match the weight of the schedule. "I can reschedule the tea."

"No," I say, pulling on my gloves. "They'll think I'm withdrawing again. I can't give them more whispers."

"Let them whisper," she mutters.

"If only it were that simple."

Our day unfolds with exhausting precision.

I walk the marble halls like a ghost inside golden skin, smiling at nobles I barely know, nodding through lectures I've heard a dozen times. My fingers blister during weaponry drills... Captain Rhord insists on perfection, and I insist on not giving him the satisfaction of seeing me fail.

Bethany trails behind me always. Not like a servant. Like a sentry. She holds my gloves when I kneel before the Eldorian orphans. She shields me from Lord Halric's wandering eyes during lunch. She pretends not to notice when I choke back tears during the choir's rehearsal of my mother's funeral hymn.

She's seen me cry. Once. The day they laid my mother in the stone tomb by the reflecting pools.

She didn't speak. Just stood beside me in the cold, holding my hand so tightly I forgot I was royalty for a moment.

The afternoon fades into evening without pause. My limbs ache. My thoughts race. My soul is tired.

But Bethany, damn her... still has energy.

She tugs at the hem of my sleeve as I linger too long in the corridor outside the memorial hall. "Seraphina, you don't have to carry it all alone."

I give her a look. Worn. Hollowed. "But I do, Beth. That's the point. No one else can."

She says nothing. Just walks beside me, shoulder brushing mine. The warmth of her presence is the only thing keeping me from splintering like the old statues crumbling in the gardens.

Tonight, we return to my chambers in silence. I collapse onto the edge of my bed, undoing the buttons at my collar with shaking fingers.

Bethany steps behind me, unlaces my corset wordlessly, lets it fall to the floor. She brushes my hair with slow, deliberate strokes. I feel like a child again.

"You've done enough today," she says.

I want to cry. I don't.

She helps me into a soft nightgown and tucks the blankets over me like she always does.

"Beth?"

She turns at the door.

"Thank you," I whisper.

Her smile is soft, wistful. "Always."

When the door shuts, I stare up at the stone ceiling, counting the cracks like stars.

My body aches from drills. My mind buzzes from politics. My heart is a silent scream in my chest.

But for now... I rest.

Because tomorrow, I must become the perfect heir again.

CHAPTER 11
WHERE SHADOWS LINGER

__BETHANY__

T he cold of morning clung to the stone corridors like breath frozen mid-whisper.

I stirred beneath my wool blanket, reluctant to leave the warmth of my cot. My chamber wasn't lavish... just a narrow bed, a modest armoire, and a single, crooked window... but it served me well enough. I sat up, combing fingers through my tangled hair, the silence around me broken only by the quiet creak of the wind outside and the occasional drip of melting frost from the eaves.

Dressing was ritual. My pale hands, still half-numb, laced the bodice of my gown with practiced ease. I secured the pin of Eldoria at my collar, a silver crescent threaded with a rose motif, then wrapped my shawl around my shoulders. The castle never truly warmed, not even by midday. The stones drank the cold and held it hostage.

As I stepped into the corridor, the scent of ash and old parchment greeted me like a familiar ghost. Servants passed in silence, nodding politely, their eyes downcast. We all moved in orbit around the same sun: *her*. Seraphina.

But before I could bathe in her fire, I had my task.

As I made my way toward the council chamber to collect the day's itinerary, my steps slowed near the war room... an involuntary reflex. I always tread a little more carefully when he was near.

Malakar.

The King's most trusted advisor. His shadow in daylight. His blade in the dark.

No man held more sway within the castle walls, save for the King himself. And if one listened closely, they might question even that.

He wasn't merely a man of court and counsel. No. Malakar was a sorcerer. One who whispered to flame and bone, whose presence darkened doorways and made the candles flicker low. The scent of smoke clung to him... always. As if the fire never quite left him.

There were rumors, of course. Whispers behind closed doors and nervous glances exchanged by the younger scribes. That Malakar had been trained by the Witch of the Eldorian Forest herself. That she had poured her blackened wisdom into him like wine into a chalice, and he drank every drop.

I wasn't sure I believed all of it.

But I believed enough.

Everyone in Eldoria knew of Elysandra.

They had to. She was etched into the very bones of the realm.

She was more legend than flesh. A ghost in the treetops. The last thing you saw before your breath left you.

They say she's lived for nine hundred years.

That she doesn't age.

That she can bend time and shape fate and speak to the dead.

Children are warned not to stray too close to the tree line, else the Witch will come and snatch them up. Ferry them through the trees and across the Veil. Feed them to the forest to keep it alive.

It sounds like a tale... until you see it.

The trees.

Always green.

Always lush.

Even now, as frost creeps across the fields and the river's edge freezes solid, the forest blooms. As if untouched by the seasons. Or perhaps feeding off them.

And then... there are the sightings.

Every few years, a soldier stationed near the perimeter comes stumbling back to the gates, pale and trembling. Swearing he saw a woman in the woods. Cloaked in black. Skin like marble. Hair like wildfire.

Emerald eyes.

Eyes that could peel the soul from your spine.

Some say she's beautiful beyond compare. Others say her beauty is a curse, too sharp, too perfect, like a blade wrapped in silk.

No one dares go in after her.

Not even Malakar.

And yet, he carries her teachings in every motion of his hand.

He's a living extension of her will. Whatever bond they forged—mentor and pupil, sorcerer and witch—it bound him tightly. And we're the ones who have to live with the consequences.

As I neared the door to the council chamber, my stomach twisted. Not from fear, exactly. But from that deep, instinctual sense of knowing...

Malakar already knew I was coming.

Malakar's study was tucked near the war chambers, a room that always felt like it breathed with secrets. When I knocked, the door creaked open on its own, a habit of his I found theatrical and annoying.

He barely looked up from his quillwork. "Bethany," he said flatly, sliding a parchment across the table. "Today's itinerary. She is not to be late for the House Council this time."

"She won't be," I replied, and his skeptical grunt was all the thanks I'd get.

Clutching the rolled parchment, I made my way up the spiral stairs to the high wing, where the air felt thinner and the halls were wide enough for sunlight to get lost in.

Seraphina's chambers were silent, but the moment I knocked and entered, that silence turned sacred.

She stood near the window, hair still unbound, brushing it in long strokes. Light spilled across her skin like the gods themselves had paused to admire her. That midnight black hair of hers caught fire in the light... untamed, beautiful, something between rebellion and royalty. Her nightgown clung to the soft curves of her frame, the fabric pale against her skin, like parchment yet unmarked.

"Morning, Bethany," she said, voice still thick with sleep.

There was no one like her. Not in Eldoria. Not in the world.

I often wondered if she truly knew how radiant she was, not just beautiful, but terrifying in that beauty. A living contradiction of duty and desire. She made me feel like I was always standing too close to a flame but never close enough to burn.

"You'll want to hurry," I said gently, trying not to sound like I was scolding her. "Malakar's already breathing fire."

Seraphina smirked, unbothered. "Let him choke on his own smoke."

I smiled despite myself. Of course she would say that.

I helped her dress, layering her in silks the color of plum and frost. As I fastened the buttons at her back, I caught myself pausing... watching the line of her shoulder blade, the slope of her neck, the way she tilted her head ever so slightly to the side as I adjusted her collar. She was beauty personified. And I was proud to call her my closest friend.

I handed her the parchment. She glanced over it with a sigh.

"Breakfast with the House Council. Training inspection. The visiting noble from Aereth. And of course," she said, glancing at me with a grin, "the endlessly thrilling embroidery hour with Lady Velline."

"Riveting," I deadpanned. "Truly, the highlight."

We both laughed.

But then it happened.

As I moved to lace the final ribbon at her sleeve, my vision blurred. Just for a heartbeat... maybe less. But in that instant, something else came rushing in. A flash of rope. Pale wood. Silence that screamed.

I froze. My breath caught in my throat.

It passed as quickly as it came, leaving behind only a chill coiled around my spine like a serpent.

Seraphina turned to look at me. "Beth? Are you alright?"

I blinked, forcing a smile. "Yes. Just a... draft."

Her gaze lingered on me a moment longer, suspicious. But then she turned away, back toward the mirror.

I glanced upward.

Toward the rafters.

There was nothing there... just old beams and shadows. Still... something inside me recoiled. A pulse of dread I couldn't explain. I shook it off.

"Come," I said, clearing my throat. "If we don't hurry, Malakar's going to chew steel."

We walked together out into the corridor, her arm brushing mine as we went.

Another day of duty. Another day of keeping my dearest friend on task, and what a duty that is at times.

The castle pulsed with motion as we moved through it, like a great beast stretching awake, half-starved and restless. Servants hurried down corridors with folded linens or trays of tepid tea. Guards rotated at their posts with grim, unreadable faces. No one met Seraphina's eyes directly, but I saw the way they looked at her when she passed. With reverence. With fear. With hope so desperate it hurt to see.

She bore it well or at least pretended to. A tight smile. A nod. A cool grace that never cracked in public. I knew better. I'd seen her break.

The House Council was already seated by the time we entered the eastern solar. The men stood when she approached, their bowed heads disguising their contempt... or their awe. Maybe both.

The meeting was more of the same. Allocation reports. Dwindling grain. A shipment from the eastern isles delayed again. Malakar pacing at her side like a tethered hawk, his voice sharp, his eyes sharper.

I stood behind her chair as always, silent and still, my presence barely acknowledged. But that was fine. I preferred to watch. To listen.

And I heard everything.

Especially when they didn't mean to be heard.

Later, after embroidery with Lady Velline had drained what was left of Seraphina's patience, and mine... we passed the southern atrium, where the noblewomen often gathered for tea and polished gossip.

"... I'm telling you, my cousin in Varthridge says the front lines haven't moved in a fortnight," one whispered, fanning herself despite the cool air.

"Stalemate?" another asked.

"Starvation," the first woman corrected. "Our supply lines are stretched too thin. Half the soldiers are sick. The other half are deserting."

A third voice chimed in, older and bitter. "They say Morvath is just as bad. Kael the Ruthless has bled his own men dry. Sacrificed entire battalions for a single outpost."

"Is it true he decapitates prisoners himself?"

"They say he hangs the heads along the valley walls. Sends the bodies back in pieces."

I felt Seraphina stiffen beside me. Her fingers clenched the scroll she carried. I said nothing, just walked a step closer to her side.

"They call him the Butcher of the North now," the older woman continued. "Cut through three legions in one night. No mercy. No survivors."

A younger girl at the edge of the circle let out a nervous laugh. "Sounds more beast than man."

"Exactly," the older one snapped. "He's not a king... he's a demon given skin."

We kept walking, but the words lingered like smoke in our lungs. Seraphina didn't speak until we reached the northern courtyard.

"Rumors," she said flatly.

"Maybe," I offered. "But even shadows are born of something real."

She didn't answer. Just kept walking.

The rest of the day blurred into routine. Inspection rounds. Lunch in silence. A training demonstration that left Seraphina visibly unimpressed. The nobleman from Aereth arrived late and stinking of fermented fruit, and she suffered through his fawning with the patience of a saint and the soul of a dagger.

By the time the sun dipped behind the ramparts, the castle felt colder than it had in the morning.

We returned to her chambers in near silence, both of us worn thin.

Seraphina sat before the mirror as I unpinned her hair. The strands slid through my fingers like silk as I combed them gently. She stared at her reflection, but not at her face, no, her eyes wandered to the empty space behind her, as if she saw something coming for her in the dark.

I wanted to say something. Anything.

Instead, I folded her nightgown across the edge of her bed and helped her undress in silence. When her back was to me, I noticed a small bruise just below her ribcage.

Training again, probably. She never complained, even when she bled.

She changed and slipped beneath the covers without a word.

I moved to extinguish the lantern by her bedside.

"Bethany," she said suddenly, voice quiet.

I turned. "Yes?"

"You don't have to stay."

"I know," I replied. But I didn't move.

For a moment, neither did she.

Then, slowly, she closed her eyes.

I blew out the light and let the room fall to shadows.

And even in the dark, I watched over her.

Like always.

CHAPTER III
HEIR OF DUTY

SERAPHINA

T he sun set behind the distant mountains of Eldoria, casting long shadows across frozen, snow-covered hills. The last embers of daylight bled into the sky, painting it a shade of gold that I had once found comforting. Now, it felt like the beginning of something heavy, something inevitable.

As I stood at the balcony of my chamber, my fingers traced the delicately frosted gold filigree of the railing, the cold evening air stirring my dark hair. The breeze was brisk, carrying with it a chill that sent a shiver up my spine. I breathed in the morning air, hoping it could ease the tension in my chest.

I had been groomed for this life... this very moment... since I was a child. At twelve, I had learned to sit through hours of meetings, my posture perfect, my smile polite. At sixteen, I was introduced to the intricacies of diplomacy, of alliances, of power. And now, at twenty-one, I was expected to be the future queen of Eldoria. My people needed me, my kingdom needed me, and yet, the weight of it all was suffocating.

With a soft sigh, I turned away from the window and walked toward the mirror across the room. The reflection that greeted me was one I knew too well: a woman, poised and graceful, dressed in an elegant gown of midnight blue. The corset-style bodice hugged my slender frame, and the flowing skirt rippled with each movement. My dark hair, carefully styled into loose waves, framed my face, making my striking green eyes the focal point. I was beautiful, a fact that my advisors never failed to remind me.

But there was a hollowness in those eyes, a sadness I had learned to mask over the years. I was not merely a princess; I was a symbol, a political tool to further my kingdom's interests. My father's expectations loomed like an unshakable mountain.

"Your Highness, the council awaits you," came the soft voice of my maid, Bethany, interrupting my thoughts.

I turned to find her standing in the doorway, her expression respectful but laced with concern. Bethany had been with me since childhood, and she knew me better than anyone. She often saw the cracks in the mask I wore.

"Thank you, Bethany," I said, my voice steady. I had learned to sound composed, even when my insides were in turmoil. I glanced at my reflection once more. "I suppose duty calls."

Bethany nodded; her soft features etched with a sadness of her own. "If I may, Your Highness, you don't have to do this. You are not bound by these choices. You still have time."

Her words, though kind, stung. Time. What was time to me? I had no time to live for myself. Eldoria needed its heir. And the kingdoms surrounding us needed their alliances.

"Let's not delay." I smiled at Bethany, though the effort felt hollow. "I will meet them in the council chamber."

The long corridors of Eldoria's castle echoed with the sound of my footsteps as I made my way toward the council chambers. Each step felt like a step closer to something I had no say in. The distant rumble of thunder sounded in the distance, reminding me that the tension between Eldoria and the neighboring kingdom of Morvath was as persistent as the storms that often ravaged our lands.

The kingdom of Morvath had been our enemy for as long as I could remember, ruled by the notorious and feared Kael, a man as brutal as the northern winds and as relentless as the wars he led. I had heard stories about him: how he could crush an opponent's skull with a single blow, how he commanded his people with an iron fist, how his very name struck terror into the hearts of those who crossed him.

My duty to Eldoria, to its people, to my father, was to negotiate peace with him... Kael, the barbarian.

The council chamber doors opened before me, and the sound of murmurs and hushed conversations stopped. The men and women of the council rose as I entered, their expressions a mix of respect and anticipation. I had been conditioned to this my entire life, but as I stood there, at the head of the long table, I couldn't help but feel small under their gaze.

"Your Highness," my father's voice boomed from the head of the table, cutting through my thoughts. King Solric, the ruler of Eldoria, was a man of few words and many commands. His deep voice was a reflection of the power he wielded, but his eyes, the same cold, calculating eyes I had inherited... never showed warmth.

I curtsied before him. "Father," I greeted.

"Sit, Seraphina," he said, motioning toward the seat beside him. As I took my place, I couldn't help but notice the subtle shift in the air, the quiet expectation. The weight of my future rested heavily upon my shoulders.

"We've received a message from Morvath," said Lord Caldor, the kingdom's top military adviser. His voice was grave as he unrolled the letter, and I saw the familiar seal of the Morvath kingdom embossed on the parchment. "Kael wishes to discuss terms of a truce."

A murmur rippled through the council. A truce? The words felt strange. No one truly believed that peace could come between our kingdoms, not after the years of bloodshed, not after the raids that had scarred our people. But here it was... a chance for diplomacy.

"We cannot trust him," Malakar, my father's most loyal adviser, interjected. "He is a barbarian. He only seeks to conquer. This armistice is nothing but a trap."

My father's lips curled into a tight smile. "We cannot ignore an opportunity for peace, no matter how fleeting. Prepare Seraphina for the negotiations."

My heart skipped. The negotiations? Of course. This was my role, my duty, to fix the broken peace, to end the suffering. I had been groomed for this my entire life.

"Yes, Father," I replied, my voice steady despite the fluttering in my chest.

That night, as the final embers of the council's discussion faded, I retired to my chambers. My thoughts lingered on Kael the ruthless, cold leader of the enemy kingdom. The thought of meeting him sent a chill down my spine, a mixture of dread and curiosity.

I had never met Kael in person, but I knew his reputation well. It had been ingrained in me since childhood. And yet, there was something about the very idea of him that stirred a strange feeling in my chest... something I couldn't name.

"Your Highness," Bethany's voice broke through my reverie as she entered the room. "Are you well?"

I turned to face her, offering a weak smile. "I suppose I'm ready."

"For the negotiations?"

I hesitated, my gaze dropping to the floor. "I have no choice. It is my duty."

Bethany's soft gaze was filled with empathy. She could see the turmoil behind my eyes. "You don't have to do this, Seraphina. There is still time to make another choice."

But I knew that wasn't true. I could not turn my back on Eldoria, not when the fate of so many rested on my shoulders.

"You speak as though there's another option," I said, my voice quieter than I intended.

"There is always a choice," Bethany replied softly, but she did not push further. She knew that once I had made up my mind, nothing could sway me.

As I lay in bed that night, my thoughts turned again to Kael. The enemy leader who would soon be standing before me. I had no idea how our meeting would go, what he would say or do. But one thing was clear: this meeting could change everything.

And though I didn't yet know it, the moment I laid eyes on him, my world would begin to crumble.

CHAPTER IV
KAEL THE RUTHLESS

KAEL

The wind hit me like a wall as I stepped out of the command tent, sharp and cold, biting into the leather of my armor. The familiar scent of saltwater hung in the air, mingling with the earthy undertones of fresh blood. The battlefield had been quiet for hours now, the faint sounds of dying embers crackling around the perimeter of the camp. I didn't flinch at the sight of the fallen soldiers, nor at the bodies being gathered by my men. Blood had soaked into the earth for years, and I was as much a part of it as the land we fought for.

I stood tall, my back straight despite the weight of exhaustion, my gaze locked on the horizon, where the distant mountains of Eldoria loomed. That kingdom... their kingdom, had been our rival for as long as I could remember. Eldoria, with its wealth, its grand history, and its false sense of peace, was everything that Morvath was not. I had made it my life's mission to change that.

I ran a hand over my thick, dark beard, the salt of the air making it stiff against my palm. The tattoos that covered my arms, my chest, my stomach, they were a map of my journey, a testament to the battles I had fought and the men I had led. Every mark told a story of conquest, of pain, and of blood. The ink had long since become a part of me, woven into my very skin, just like the war that had become my life.

Morvath, my kingdom... my legacy, was built from the very fires of war. I lead my people not through charisma, not through kindness, but with a hardened soul. I had made my name known across the lands through bloodshed. I had become a force to be feared and respected. For all the years of our existence, we had been pushed into the shadows, dismissed as barbarians, nothing more than an irritation to the more civilized kingdoms of the world.

But I knew the truth, what they called barbarism was the will to survive in a world that had long since forgotten what strength was.

Strength. That was my kingdom's currency. There is no place for weakness in Morvath. In the heat of battle, you either fought, or you died. There is no middle ground.

But it wasn't just power I fought for. It wasn't just the lands that I wanted. I fought for a future where we wouldn't have to hide, where we could stand tall and demand respect. I would carve that future with my own hands, even if it meant breaking every rule of diplomacy along the way.

It wasn't often that I sent someone to speak for me. Morvath had never been one to engage in petty negotiations. Our enemies had always learned to fear the sound of our war drums. But there was something about Eldoria, something about their princess that stirred a different kind of tension within me.

After the most recent skirmish, my advisers and I had discussed the possibility of a truce. Eldoria had suffered heavy losses but so had we. The bloodshed had reached a point where even I could feel the strain. My people were tired, and I was tired. But I would never show it. Weakness was never an option.

The time had come for diplomacy... for negotiation.

"Send an emissary," I had told my most trusted lieutenant, Alistair, earlier that evening. His large, muscular frame was like a shadow beside me as we stood overlooking the battlefield, both of us silent for a long moment.

"Who do you think will listen to our terms?" Alistair had asked, his voice rough, steeped in the same wariness that had been etched into his face over the years.

"The Eldorian's have their King, but it's the princess that concerns me," I replied, my voice low. "Seraphina. The heiress. She's the one who will rule that kingdom when her father's reign ends. She's the one who holds the future in her hands."

Alistair had nodded, already knowing what I meant. I didn't trust that delicate, polished princess any more than I trusted the rest of Eldoria's elite, but I knew she was the key. If I could speak with her, perhaps there was a way to bend the kingdom to my will without the need for more bloodshed.

That night, by the dim light of a flickering fire, I had written my message. The letter was simple, the tone direct, as cold as the winter winds that howled through the hills. It was a call for diplomacy, yes, but it was also a warning.

I couldn't afford to appear weak, not even in a diplomatic setting. I knew they wouldn't trust me. That was fine. I didn't need their trust. What I needed was an armistice, a chance to regroup, to rebuild, and to plan the next move in a war that had lasted far too long. If they wanted peace, they would have to earn it. So, I wrote.

To the Council of Eldoria,

The endless bloodshed between our peoples has gone on long enough, and while I would prefer to conquer your lands outright, I am offering you a rare chance at diplomacy. Do not mistake this gesture for weakness, it is born from pragmatism, not mercy.

I propose a meeting on neutral ground to discuss terms that might bring an end to this war. Bring your leaders and those capable of making decisions, for I have no patience for politics or delays. Should peace prove unattainable, the Ironclad Dominion will continue its advance, and your cities will burn beneath our blades.

Know this: If I detect even the faintest hint of treachery or deceit, I will personally ensure that your precious princess's head is sent back to you on a pike. You will have no place to hide, no walls high enough, no armies strong enough to stop me from bringing the fury of my people upon you.

The decision is yours, peace or annihilation. I will await your response on neutral ground outside the southern border of your territory in three days' time.

Kael of the Ironclad Dominion

I handed the message to Marek, a trusted messenger from my camp, a man whose loyalty was unquestionable. He was quick, and he knew the route to Eldoria. I had no doubts that the message would reach them within days.

"Deliver this to Seraphina's court in Eldoria. Let them know that I am coming to speak of terms, in neutral territory." My voice was firm, and Marek understood what I meant. Neutral ground meant that there would be no traps, no underhanded games.

Marek nodded silently and took the sealed message. "It will be done, my lord."

Once Marek had departed, the weight of the coming meeting settled on me like a cloak. There would be no more battles today, no more bloodshed. In less than a weeks' time, we would meet in neutral territory, where Eldoria's representatives would be waiting. The thought didn't sit easily with me. The politics of it all, it was a game, a dance, a farce. But it was one I had to play, and so I would.

Later that evening, as the moon began to rise over the northern hills, I prepared for the journey to meet the Eldorian's. My camp was already buzzing with activity, the soldiers moving with practiced precision to ready the tents, pack provisions, and ensure we were fully equipped for the diplomatic meeting.

Alistair was at my side once again, his face hard as granite, as always. "Are you truly going to meet them, Kael? After all we've done to them? It's a dangerous game you're playing."

I met his gaze. "I'm not playing a game, Alistair. I'm making sure this kingdom, my kingdom, survives. We survive through strength, but sometimes strength must be tempered by reason."

The sound of the horses being prepared reached my ears, and I motioned toward the stables. "Prepare your men. We leave at first light."

Kael The Ruthless

CHAPTER V

HIDDEN SANCTUARY

SERAPHINA

I never intended to become a ghost in my own castle. But some nights... I need to disappear. The stone beneath my boots is slick with mist as I slip past the chapel, lantern swinging at my side like a fragile heartbeat. I know this path. I could walk it blindfolded. Past the mausoleum, where my ancestors sleep in their cold stone beds. Past the statue of the weeping angel no one visits anymore.

The guards don't stop me... they never do. I think they know better than to ask questions when I wear this face. The one that says I will shatter if they speak. My cloak is too thin for the wind tonight. It snakes beneath the hem and claws at my ribs like fingers from the grave, but I press on, deeper into the dark, until I see the gate.

Twisted iron. Rusted hinges. Half-consumed by ivy. The garden. It's nearly gone now. My mother's sanctuary, forgotten by time and devoured by nature. We used to come here in the early mornings, when the sun burned the dew into steam and the roses bloomed wild and shameless. Now? Now it smells of damp rot and regret. I push open the gate. It groans like it remembers me. Or maybe it resents me for coming back. The vines have swallowed everything. The marble bench is cracked, moss growing along its spine like a wound that never healed. The fountain is dry. The statues wept themselves smooth years ago.

And yet...

This is the only place that feels honest. I lower the lantern and kneel beside the bench, pulling the small spade from beneath my cloak. I always bring it, though I tell no one why. Bethany used to ask. She doesn't anymore. Maybe she's afraid of the answer. The earth is damp and soft beneath my hands. Familiar. It gives easily, like it's used to swallowing things I can't hold anymore.

Tonight, I bury a ribbon. Blue silk, frayed at the edges. My mother used to braid it into my hair when I was small. She said it made me look like the sea. I never understood what she meant until I saw the ocean for the first time and realized it was both beautiful and endless, and always just out of reach. I lay the ribbon gently into the hollow I've carved and cover it with earth, pressing it flat with my palms. My fingers tremble. Not from cold. I exhale, long and quiet, and let my weight settle into the dirt. The lantern casts a pale halo over the broken stone and tangled vines. Everything looks softer in this light. Even the decay. "I miss you," I whisper, to no one and to her and to everything I lost the day they lowered her into the ground.

She would hate what I've become. She would hate the way I smile and lie and kill with words sharp as razors. The way I wear the crown like a noose. The way I crave freedom like a starving thing. I've often thought about how I can manage to be me and who I am expected to be. I don't think I can. "I don't know how to be both," I say aloud. "The ruler they want and the woman I am." The vines don't answer. The earth doesn't care. The garden isn't here to absolve me.

I reach into my cloak again and pull out an apple. Red. Polished. Perfect. A symbol of sin and knowledge. A gift. A warning. I place it beside the ribbon's shallow grave. There's something absurd about it... laying fruit like an offering to a ghost. But grief doesn't care about logic. And I have no prayers left. "I want freed," I admit, my voice cracking in the stillness. "And I want her. And I want out. I want more than duty and bloodlines and whispers behind my back."

The moon is high above the trees now, casting silver bars through the fog like a cage. "I can't keep doing this," I say to the night. But I will. Because I always do. The crunch of gravel makes me freeze. I don't turn. I know who it is. Bethany. She lingers at the edge of the gate like a shadow unsure of its shape.

"You shouldn't be here," I say without looking up.

"Neither should you," she replies.

I hear the gate click shut behind her. Her footsteps are soft. Careful. She walks like she doesn't want to disturb the dead. She sits beside me on the bench. Close, but not touching. The silence stretches between us like a string pulled taut.

"This was hers, wasn't it?" she asks after a while. I nod.

"Everything good in me lived here once." Bethany runs her fingers along the bench's edge. "She must've loved it."

"She did." My voice thickens. "She said it was a place where nothing evil could follow us." Bethany's lips curl into a bitter smile. "Looks like it didn't last." I laugh, but it's a dry, hollow thing.

"Nothing ever does." I glance at her then, and she's already watching me. Really watching. Like she's trying to memorize the shape of my soul.

"I miss her," I say, surprising myself. "But more than that, I miss who I was when she was alive." Bethany's hand brushes mine. Warm. Steady. Hesitant.

"You're still her," she says softly. I shake my head.

"No. I'm what's left after the fire." She doesn't argue. Maybe she knows better. Maybe she's burned too. I turn to her fully, the fog curling around us like a secret. "If I asked you to run away with me," I say quietly, "what would you do?" Bethany's breath catches. Her eyes flick to mine, searching for the lie.

"Where would we go?"

"Anywhere but here."

She swallows. "And what would we be?" I look down at our hands, mine stained with dirt and memory. Hers clean. For now.

"Free," I whisper. Bethany says nothing. But she doesn't pull away. And that's almost enough to make me believe. Almost. But not quite. Because the moment breaks. It always does. And I remember the weight of the crown. The blood in the halls. The eyes that watch. The choices I've already made. I pull my hand back. Stand. Adjust the cloak. Bury the feeling. "Thank you for coming," I say, voice cold again. Mask restored. Bethany doesn't try to stop me. I walk away from the garden. From her. From the girl I used to be. The fog swallows everything behind me. And still, I feel the dirt under my nails. Still, I feel the ribbon in the ground. Still, I feel the weight of the apple. Rotting, just beneath the surface.

CHAPTER VI
THE WARLORD AWAITS

SERAPHINA

The fire had burned low, casting faint flickers of amber across the stone walls. Shadows stretched and curled like specters, restless and hungry. I lay awake, staring at the ceiling, feeling the weight of the coming dawn pressing against my chest like a phantom's hand. I was to meet Kael of Morvath. His name alone carried weight, whispered in fear across war-torn lands. A barbarian, they called him. A ruthless conqueror, a monster cloaked in flesh.

And yet, I was to face him... alone. I exhaled slowly, pressing my fingers against my forehead. The weight of the crown that had not yet touched my head was already suffocating. A knock at my door jolted me from my thoughts.

Bethany.

"Come in," I called with a cracked voice, already knowing she would. She entered with a silver tray; the scent of steeped black tea laced with honey curling through the air. Her golden braid rested over her shoulder, blue eyes immediately scanning my face.

"You didn't sleep."

"Observant as ever," I muttered. Bethany set the tray down with an exasperated sigh. "Seraphina." I ignored her, wrapping my arms around my knees. "What if he refuses peace? What if this is all for nothing?" Bethany hesitated, then sat beside me on the bed, her voice softer than before. "What if it's not?" I didn't answer. Because I wasn't sure I wanted to know.

BETHANY

I had known this girl... this woman, since childhood. When she bled, I was the one who wiped away the crimson. When she wept, I was the one who held her through the storm. And now? I was meant to watch her walk into a warlord's grasp, alone in the middle of a battlefield. The thought made my stomach churn. I picked up her cloak, running my fingers over the embroidered crest of Eldoria. "You'll let me come with you," I said finally, turning back to her. She frowned. "What? I'm not staying behind," I pressed. "Where you go, I go." She opened her mouth, perhaps to argue, perhaps to refuse, but she hesitated. Because she knew I was right. A long silence passed. Then, finally, she exhaled.

"Fine."

Seraphina

The corridors of Castle Eldor were quiet at this hour, filled with the hush of early morning. The faint glow of torchlight flickered against the stone walls as Bethany and I made our way toward the courtyard, the cold seeping in through the grand archways. Then, as we rounded a corner, I saw her. A woman, or perhaps just a trick of the torchlight, stood at the far end of the hall, her presence nearly swallowed by shadows. But what I noticed first wasn't her figure, nor the way she stood so still it was unnerving. It was her hair. Fire-red, spilling in waves down her back. I stopped abruptly, my breath catching in my throat. Bethany followed my gaze.

"What is it?" I blinked. The hallway was empty.

"... Nothing," I murmured, but a shiver crept up my spine.

Bethany

The air was brutally cold, biting at my exposed skin as we made our way to the stables. Snow had begun to fall lightly, dusting the stone pathways in white. The Knights of Luminara, handpicked from the royal guard... were already mounted and waiting, their presence a reminder of just how serious this was. Seraphina's mare was readied; her cloak fastened tightly over her shoulders. But as she reached for the reins, I caught a glimpse of something. A woman stood at the tree line beyond the castle gates. Red hair, eyes that seemed to gleam even in the dim morning light. I grabbed Seraphina's arm. "You see her, don't you?" I whispered. Her fingers curled into my sleeve. And then... she was gone.

SERAPHINA

The wind howled as we rode, a sharp contrast to the silence between us. The snow-covered plains stretched endlessly ahead, a vast, empty expanse. The Knights of Luminara rode behind Bethany and me in formation, their presence a cold comfort. But my mind was elsewhere. On him. On the warlord who waited just beyond the horizon. I had spent years picturing the enemy as faceless. A shadow. A force. But soon, I would look into his eyes. And I feared that whatever I saw there... I wouldn't be able to look away.

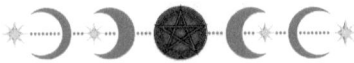

BETHANY

The land between our camp and his was barren, untouched by war but heavy with the weight of it. No banners flew here. No fires burned. Just empty snow and silence. We dismounted as we reached our tent, standing just at the edge of the battlefield, directly across from Kael's. I pulled my cloak tighter, scanning the distant tree line.

"I don't like this." Seraphina exhaled, brushing the snow from her sleeves.

"Neither do I." From this vantage point, I could see Kael's tent, nestled in the woods like a beast lurking in wait. I felt like a lamb standing at the edge of a wolf's den. And somehow, I knew... the wolf had already caught our scent.

CHAPTER VII

DIPLOMATIC SOLUTIONS

SERAPHINA

T he cold bit into my skin as I stood just outside my tent, starting across the snow-blanketed field. Bethany stood at my side; her usual expression of nervous anticipation etched on her face. Two of the Knights of Luminara, ever vigilant, flanked us silently, their gleaming armor reflecting the faint light of the overcast sky. The icy air carried a foreboding weight, and when a delicate snowflake landed on my cheek, a shiver coursed down my spine; a warning, perhaps, of what lay ahead. Through the flurry of snow, I squinted toward the enemy's tent. It rested at the field's edge, nestled ominously within the wood line.

My breath hitched as something stirred from the tent. I narrowed my eyes, trying to discern what it was. A figure emerged, a man on horseback carrying a banner of peace. The rider approached slowly, the steady crunch of snow beneath his horse's hooves breaking the silence. As he halted a few feet from us, I raised my gaze to him. He was easy on the eyes, strong in stature, with stoic allure. His chiseled features were framed by the ruggedness of his fur-lined cloak. He finally spoke, his voice deep and commanding.

"I am Alistair, second in command of the armies of the Free Clans of Morvath, second in line to the Ironclad Dominion." I dipped into a graceful curtsey, offering a small, polite smile.

"I am Seraphina, Princess of Eldoria and heir to the throne, I am pleased to make your acquaintance."

Bethany, ever proper, mirrored my gesture, her expression a mixture of respect and unease. Alistair let out a grunt, the condensation from his breath forming a plume in the freezing air.

"My Lord, Kael, awaits your arrival. Follow me." Turning his horse with practiced ease, Alistair began trotting across the field. I gathered the hem of my dress to avoid dragging it through the snow and stepped cautiously into the hoofprints he left behind. Each step seemed heavier than the last, the biting wind slicing through my cloak. As we neared the tent, the wind picked up, howling like a ghost. Alistair dismounted with fluidity, tying his horse's reins to a low-hanging branch. He motioned for us to follow as he pulled back the tent flap, holding it open with an expectant look on his face.

"Stay here," I instructed my guards, my tone firm. Their protests were met with a raised hand. "I will let you know if I need you." Bethany's eyes widened with alarm.

"M'Lady, do you think that wise?" I gave her a calm, reassuring glance.

"I am not here to show force, Bethany. I am here to negotiate peace." I stepped forward, pausing at the threshold to draw a deep breath before ducking under the flap. The warmth inside the tent was immediate and enveloping, a stark contrast to the icy chill outside. A fire burned in the center, its flames casting flickering shadows on the fur-lined walls. There he was.

Kael.

He sat on a makeshift throne, his imposing frame radiating power. His long, dark hair fell in loose waves, two braids framing his chiseled face. Piercing, ice-cold eyes locked onto mine, never wavering. His dark beard accentuated the sharpness of his jawline, and the sheer size of him was overwhelming... his fur and leather armor exuding raw, unrefined strength. My knees threatened to buckle under his gaze. My mouth opened to speak, but no words came. Bethany, sensing my struggle, stepped forward.

"May I present Seraphina, Princess of Eldoria, M'Lord?" Her words seemed to break the spell, and I managed a polite curtsey.

Kael's lips twitched into the barest hint of a smile, though his gaze remained unyielding.

"Yes," he drawled, his voice low and rumbling, "you may present her to me." His words struck me to my core, igniting a chill that rippled down my spine.

"I am Kael, leader of the Free Clans of Morvath, King to my people." The weight of his voice struck me like a blow, and I struggled to steady myself. He reached out his hand and pointed to a bench that sat in front of the fire as if to tell me to take a seat. I obediently took my seat on the bench by the fire. I silently cursed myself for complying so readily, but his presence was magnetic... an anchor I couldn't seem to break free of.

What in the fuck is wrong with me? Why did I listen and obey so quickly?

"I am here to discuss the terms of an armistice," I said, forcing my voice to remain steady. Kael leaned forward, his eyes narrowing.

"There is no need for pleasantries, Princess. We both know this isn't a grand ceremony." His words were sharp, grating against my royal decorum. "Your Kingdom," he continued, "is corrupt. You may not see it yet, but the truth is there, plain as day." Anger flared in me, hot and unforgiving. I stood up and began to pace the floor in defiance.

"I have seen no evidence of corruption in my kingdom. How dare you make such accusations without proof?" Kael rose from his seat, his towering form casting a long shadow. Slowly, deliberately, he approached me. His voice dropped to a dangerous murmur.

"The proof is for you to uncover, Princess. It matters little to me whether you believe it or not. What matters is that I have presented you with that truth and I have come here to discuss my terms." My defiance surged. Without thinking, I swung a fist at him. Kael caught my wrist effortlessly, his grip unyielding. His proximity overwhelmed me, his presence suffocating yet intoxicating. Kael stepped forward pushing me to step backwards as he approached. Before I knew it, I was pressed up against a stack of crates. He gave me a smug smile as he pulled a dagger from its sheath and firmly pressed it against my throat. As he did, I let out a slight moan.

Moaned? How in the hells can I enjoy this sort of barbarism?

"One more act of aggression," he growled, as he pressed the cold steel of the dagger further into my throat, "and I will send your pretty little head back to your father." As he finished making his demand, he turned my wrist loose from his grip. He reached down to grab my leg right behind my knee and pulled it upwards toward him. I was stunned for a moment by his display of force. I could feel him pressing into me and it sent a fire down my spine and up my legs. I was trembling. My breath hitched as the blade kissed my skin. The sensation sent a shockwave through

71

my body... fear mingled with something I couldn't name nor yet understand. "Do you understand me, girl?" he demanded, his tone a deadly whisper. I swallowed hard, my voice barely above a whisper. The sheer commanding nature made me uncontrollably bite my lip.

"Yes, Sir." I looked over to Bethany as she stood helplessly with a terrified and shocked expression on her face. The only thing I could do was let out a smile. Kael released me abruptly, his dagger slipping away as he stepped back. My pulse thundered in my ears. I didn't want it to stop. I wanted more. I struggled to compose myself.

"Here are my terms," he said, his voice a calm storm. "I want the southern territories of Eldoria. In exchange, I will leave the rest of your kingdom untouched."

"And if these terms are refused?" I asked, my voice trembling. Kael's expression darkened, his eyes burning with ruthless intent.

"Then I will destroy you all." His words hung in the air like a death knell.

"I will present these terms to my King," I replied, standing on unsteady legs. "You will have your answer within a fortnight." Kael nodded, dismissing me with a wave of his hand. As I turned to leave, his voice stopped me cold.

"By the way, Princess," he said, his grin wicked, "I won't pretend I didn't notice how much you enjoyed our little exchange. Perhaps I should be your King." I glanced back at him, my cheeks burning as his words carved into my very soul. I offered him a faint smile before stepping out into the biting cold.

CHAPTER VIII
ASHES AND EMBERS

Kael

T he fire crackled in the center of the tent, licking upward like the breath of some ancient beast that refused to die.

I sat on the edge of the bench, elbows on my knees, staring down at my hands. Calloused. Scarred. Covered in the dust and blood of a dozen campaigns. I'd broken kingdoms with these hands.

But today they trembled.

Gods fucking help me.

She was a storm, that one. Seraphina. She entered my tent wrapped in royal silk and frost, and when she spoke... gods, when she fucking *looked* at me... it was like staring into a fire I didn't know if I wanted to burn in or extinguish.

And I can't fucking afford either. I don't think her, or her entourage noticed.

I closed my eyes and inhaled the scent of burning pine. It didn't drown out her perfume. That soft trace of rose and snowfall clung to my tunic like a curse.

This wasn't supposed to happen. She was the enemy. The daughter of the king I swore to destroy. She came into my tent with diplomacy, but her eyes said something else. And mine... my soul was already at war.

A sound outside... the wind brushing the tent flaps or maybe ghosts from my past... made me reach for my blade. But I didn't unsheathe it. I just held it across my knees, a silent prayer.

It was then that Alistair entered, his armor dusted with snow. "She's returned to her camp," he said. "No incident. She left... quieter than she arrived."

I didn't look up. "Good."

"She looked back."

My head snapped up.

Alistair studied me. "You already know what I'm going to say. This... is a mistake."

I stood. The tent suddenly felt smaller. Hotter. "It's already too late."

"Then we're all dead," he muttered, before disappearing into the cold.

I moved to the war map, the familiar lines of our world drawn in blood and ambition. My hands hovered over Eldoria. The southern territories. I traced a path with my finger. It wasn't about land anymore. It wasn't even about revenge.

She'd changed something. Rattled something loose inside me I'd buried with the charred bones of my past. And it happened... that quickly. Out of nowhere.

I remembered my father's voice, smoke in his throat, whispering for me to run as the farmhouse burned around us. *Run, Kael. Don't look back.*

But godsdammit, I *looked back.*

I'd been looking back ever since.

And now Seraphina stood there... at the center of it all. A crowned princess. A living temptation. The daughter of the kingdom that had once taken everything from me.

I should destroy her.

But the thought of never seeing her again? It was a colder fate than death.

My fists clenched.

This war was no longer for vengeance. It wasn't even for peace.

It was for her.

And if fate demanded my soul in the process... So, fucking be it.

CHAPTER IX
ASHES OF THE PAST

KAEL

The cold air bit at my skin as I stepped out of the tent, watching the Princess and her entourage disappear into the snowy haze. Her figure grew smaller, but my thoughts of her only grew larger, gnawing at the edges of my mind. Seraphina was unlike the spineless dignitaries I had encountered before. There was fire in her, though it was buried beneath layers of royal decorum.

Beside me, Alistair approached with the steady crunch of boots on snow. He stood silent for a moment, then let out a low chuckle.

"Well?" he asked, his tone laced with skepticism.

"She's not what I expected," I admitted, my voice gruff.

"She's soft. Sheltered." Alistair folded his arms. "She has no place in a battlefield, no place negotiating terms with the likes of you."

"Perhaps," I muttered, my gaze fixed on the horizon where she'd vanished. "But she isn't entirely without merit. There's something there... I can't place it yet."

Alistair raised a brow. "Just don't let that fire of hers burn you. We've seen what happens when you give monarchs the benefit of the doubt."

His words cut deeper than he knew.

"I haven't forgotten," I said flatly, turning my back to him. "Prepare the men. Whatever answer they bring, we'll be ready."

Alone in my tent once more, I sat at the center table, staring at the worn war map spread before me. The lines of terrain and markings of strategy were meant to provide clarity, yet my thoughts were anything but clear.

For years, I had fought to bring the Free Clans to power, uniting those who had suffered at the hands of kings and lords. The idea of peace should have brought relief, yet the very concept felt foreign to me.

It wasn't just mistrust... it was something deeper.

The crackling fire in the tent reminded me too much of something else, something buried in the depths of my memory. My hands clenched the edge of the table, but the past pulled me under.

I was ten years old, standing in the doorway of our tiny farm-house. My father's face was etched with worry, his calloused hands trembling as he spoke to the men at the door.

"Please," he begged, his voice breaking. "We've done all we can. The drought has been cruel this year. We don't have enough to meet the quota, but what we do have…"

The man in the fine cloak, the royal tax collector, sneered. "The king's decree does not waver, farmer. You either meet the quota or face the consequences."

"We're starving ourselves to give what little we can!" my mother cried from behind my father, clutching my younger sister to her chest. "Surely the king has mercy…"

"Enough!" barked one of the armored guards, slamming the butt of his spear into the ground.

What happened next unfolded like a nightmare. The tax collector waved his hand, and the guards pushed us back into the house. My father protested, struggling against them, but they forced the door shut and bolted it from the outside.

Through the slats of the wooden walls, I saw them douse the perimeter with oil. My heart pounded as the acrid scent filled the air.

"Father?" I whimpered.

His face was pale, but his voice was steady. "Kael, stay close to me."

A torch ignited outside, and I screamed as flames began to lick the base of the walls. Smoke crept into the room, stinging my eyes and throat. My mother clutched my sister tighter, murmuring prayers as tears streamed down her face.

"Kael!" my father shouted, grabbing my arm and pulling me toward the back of the house. "There's a hole, there, in the corner. You can fit through it."

"What about you?" I cried, my voice shrill with terror.

He knelt before me, gripping my shoulders tightly. His eyes were fierce, brimming with urgency and love.

"Kael, my boy, once you get through, keep running. Don't stop. Don't look back. Do you understand me?"

The heat was unbearable, the flames roaring as they consumed everything around us. My father shoved me toward the small hole, his voice breaking.

"I love you, son. Now go!"

Tears blurred my vision as I crawled through the narrow space, splinters biting into my palms. The smoke was suffocating, the air outside offering little relief.

I ran.

I ran as the farmhouse collapsed behind me; the screams of my family swallowed by the inferno. I ran until my legs gave out, collapsing beneath a large tree stump at the edge of a clearing.

My chest heaved with ragged sobs, my face pressed against the cold, unyielding ground. Exhaustion claimed me, and darkness followed.

The sharp crackle of the fire in the tent jolted me back to the present. My hands gripped the edge of the table so tightly that my knuckles had turned white. The war map beneath me swam into focus, the lines and markings a stark reminder of why I fought.

The kings of Eldoria and their ilk had taken everything from me. No amount of peace negotiations could erase that.

"Never again," I muttered under my breath, my resolve hardening.

I stared at the map, running my finger along the southern borders of Eldoria. If the Princess couldn't deliver the terms I demanded, there would be no more room for diplomacy.

Alistair entered the tent once more, breaking the silence.

"They may break camp and ride back to Eldoria in the morning." he reported.

I nodded; my expression grim. "Good. Let them stew on what they've seen."

"So we are to wait here for them to return with an answer?" he asked.

"Yes, but we will need resupplied if we are to be here for the next full moon." I said, my tone cold. "We may need even more supplies if they refuse our terms."

"Send a small envoy back to Morvath in the morning. Have them gather us some more supplies, put rations on standby and have reinforcements at the ready just in case. The rest of us will await Eldoria's fate."

The memory of my father's last words echoed in my mind as I turned back to the map. *Keep running, Kael. Don't look back.*

But I wasn't running anymore. The fire burned low in the center of the tent, its flickering glow casting dancing shadows on the fur-lined walls. I stretched out on my bedding, exhaustion dragging me down like an anchor. The day's events... Seraphina's fire, her defiance, and the memories stirred by her presence... My body betrayed me. My eyes grew heavy, and the rhythm of the crackling flames lulled me into the grasp of sleep.

I was ten years old again. The forest was cold, its towering trees a silent audience to my despair. My small frame ached from running, my clothes were torn and singed, and my heart felt as though it would burst from the sheer weight of loss. The world was blurry; my limbs numb as I drifted in and out of consciousness. The ground beneath me was hard and cold, the air sharp with the scent of pine and frost. A cool sensation on my forehead jolted me awake. My eyelids fluttered, and through the haze, a figure began to take shape... a woman. She was the most beautiful thing I had ever seen up to that young point in my life. Her hair was a cascade of vivid red, falling in waves that glowed even in the dim light of the forest. Her eyes, as green as polished emeralds, radiated warmth and mystery. Her soft hands held a damp cloth, gently dabbing at my brow. I jerked slightly, startled by her presence.

"Shhh," she cooed, her voice a soothing melody that seemed to calm the very air around us. "Calm down now. You're safe." Her words were strange to me, almost foreign. I blinked, trying to make sense of her sudden appearance.

"Who are you?" I croaked, my voice weak and hoarse. She smiled... a small, knowing smile that felt like the first bit of light after a storm.

"My name is Elysandra," she said continuing to dab at my forehead. "I found you lying under my tree stump." I stared at her, confusion swirling in my young mind.

"Your tree stump?"

"Yes," she replied with a soft laugh, her hand pausing briefly. "My tree stump. I am the Guardian of this forest. I am the Enchanted Witch of the Eldorian Forest." Her words didn't make sense to me, but there was something about her presence that made me feel safe, even if only for a moment. "What might your name be, little one?" she asked gently, her emerald eyes locking with mine.

"Kael," I mumbled, my voice barely a whisper.

"Kael," she repeated, as if testing the sound of it. Her lips curved into a kind smile. "A strong name." She set the cloth aside, her tone softening even further. "What on earth were you doing out here all alone in my forest?" Tears welled in my eyes as the memory of what had happened surged back with cruel clarity. I told her everything... the drought, the soldiers, the fire, and my father's last words as he pushed me through the hold to escape.

Her expression changed as I spoke, a flicker of sorrow crossing her face. When I finished, she reached out and cupped my cheek with a hand as soft as silk. "You poor boy," she murmured, her voice thick with emotion. "To endure such pain at such a young age..." I felt the weight of her words, the kindness in her touch, and for the first time since I had fled the inferno, I felt the sting of tears freely falling down my face. Elysandra's other hand brushed a strand of hair from my eyes. "You are not alone, Kael. Not anymore. I know exactly where I can take you, a place where you will be safe." Her words stirred something in me... a faint ember of hope.

"Where?" I asked, my voice trembling.

"To Morvath," she replied. "It's a hard place, but it is safe. When you're strong enough, I will take you there myself." I didn't know what Morvath was, but her calm assurance made me believe it was something good, something better than the hell I had just escaped. She smiled again, leaning in close. "I will look in on you from time to time. I will watch over you, Kael." Her words wrapped around me like a warm blanket. I didn't understand how or why, but I trusted her. She was an enigma... someone unfamiliar, yet irresistibly captivating. The world around me began to blur again, her emerald eyes the last thing I saw before the dream faded.

I woke with a sharp inhale, my body tense and the tent fire burning low beside me. The warmth of the dream lingered, but it was quickly replaced by the cold reality of the present. Elysandra. The name felt like a whisper from a life I had tried to leave behind. I hadn't seen her in a few years. Knowing what I know now, she knew everything. I didn't have to tell her my name... my story, she already knew. I wonder if she had forgotten about me. Shaking my head, I sat up from my bedding. There was no room for sentiment here. Not now. Whatever ghosts haunted me, they would have to wait. The fire crackled softly as I returned to my strategy, but in the back of my mind, the witch's emerald eyes lingered, watching.

CHAPTER X
A HEART DIVIDED

SERAPHINA

T he stone walls of Eldoria's castle felt colder than usual, their imposing presence doing little to calm my nerves. Outside, the winter sun glared off the snow, but no warmth reached the halls. I walked briskly, trying to keep my composure, though my mind was a battlefield.

Kael's voice haunted me, his piercing eyes and commanding presence invading my every thought. His words had been sharp, brutal even, the blade of his dagger on my skin was intoxicating, it all carried a strange weight that stirred something deep within me. I clenched my fists, desperate to focus on the task at hand. I had to present his terms to my father. That was all. A simple diplomatic report.

But it wasn't simple. Nothing about this was simple.

Bethany was waiting for me in my chambers, her arms crossed and her face pale with fury. The moment I closed the door she rounded on me.

"What the hell was that in the tent?" she hissed, her voice low but seething with anger.

I blinked, startled by her tone. "What do you mean?"

She threw her hands in the air, exasperated. "Don't play dumb with me, Seraphina. You know exactly what I mean! That display with Kael... You looked like his little harlot!"

The word struck me like a slap, and I recoiled, my chest tightening.

"Bethany..." I started, but she cut me off.

"No, I'm not finished!" she snapped. "Do you have any idea what it looked like? The way he touched you, the way you... God, the way you melted under his hand. You even moaned as he touched you! You might as well have been begging him to take you right there in front of everyone!"

My cheeks burned, both from shame and anger. "That is not what happened!"

Even though, that is exactly what had happened. In that moment, when Kael had me pressed up against those crates, with his dagger to my throat, my leg hiked up that seemed to wrap around him, FUCK! In that moment... He could have had me. I would have given myself to him. Even with Bethany watching, I would have given him anything he wanted. DAMNIT! I don't even know why!

"Really?" she shot back. "Because from where I was standing, it sure as hell looked like it. What would your future husband think if he saw that?"

Her words hit a raw nerve. My future husband. But I didn't care. He was just a faceless man I was meant to marry for the sake of the kingdom. A man I didn't know and didn't fucking want. I felt the tears welling in my eyes and fought to hold them back.

"I haven't given myself to any man," I said, my voice trembling. "I am still a virgin."

Bethany narrowed her eyes, her tone softening slightly but no less biting. "That may be true, but it doesn't change what it looked like. Seraphina, you're the heir to the throne. You can't—"

"Enough!" I shouted, cutting her off.

Bethany fell silent, her expression a mix of shock and guilt.

"I didn't mean for any of it to happen," I said, my voice breaking. "It was like... Like I lost control of myself. I don't know what came over me."

Bethany sighed, running a hand through her hair. Seraphina, you're my best friend. I'll follow you through the fires of hell if that's where you lead, but you have to understand how this looks. I'm confused, too. I just..."

She trailed off, her anger fading into concern.

I stepped closer to her, placing a hand on her arm. "I owe you my allegiance as much as you owe me yours. You are my closest confidante, Bethany, and I beg you, please don't speak of this to anyone. I need time to sort this out."

Bethany hesitated, then nodded reluctantly. "Alright. I'll keep my mouth shut. But Seraphina... Be careful. Whatever this is, don't let it consume you."

Her words lingered as I turned away, my mind spinning with doubt and fear. It had already consumed me. I'm meant to be something I don't want to be. I wanted Kael. Even though I couldn't understand how or why, but I had to see him again.

The throne room was as intimidating as ever, its towering columns and intricate tapestries serving as a constant reminder of my duty. My father sat on the gilded throne, his sharp eyes studying me as I approached.

"Well?" he said, his voice deep and commanding. "What terms did this barbarian offer?"

I took a deep breath, forcing my voice to remain steady.

"Kael demands the southern territories of Eldoria in exchange for peace. He has promised to leave the rest of the kingdom untouched if his terms are met. He awaits our answer within a fortnight."

My father leaned back, stroking his beard thoughtfully. "And what kind of man is he? Was he the barbarian the rumors make him out to be, or did he show some semblance of civility?"

My breath hitched, my mind betraying me. Images of Kael flooded my thoughts... his piercing eyes, the rough strength of his hands, the low rumble of his voice. My knees felt weak, my heart pounding in my chest.

FUCK! Why in the fuck do I feel this way!? Why can I not hold it together when that man enters my thoughts!?

I shifted my weight, sliding my knees back and forth in an effort to compose myself. It only made things worse. I was hoping it would have kept my mind on what my father had asked me, but all it did was squeeze the lips of my pussy together around my already swollen clit in a rubbing motion. Heat pooled in my core, spreading until I felt a mortifying wetness trickling down my thighs. All it did was make me wet as fuck thinking about him. If I kept rubbing my legs together, I was going to cum.

Shit! Shit! Shit! I had clenched my fists at my side frozen in panic.

"Seraphina?" my father said, his tone sharp.

I snapped my gaze back to him, realizing I hadn't answered his question. "He is... Complicated," I managed, my voice barely above a whisper.

Before he could press further, my father changed the subject abruptly. "I've decided to host a formal ball to announce your engagement. It's time the kingdom sees you as the future queen you are."

Really? A fucking ball? Out of all the things that are happening right now... He wants to host a fucking ball!? To announce an engagement that I wasn't the least interested in of all things. All I can honestly think about is I am so glad he changed the subject. I don't know how much more I could handle if I didn't get a reprieve from Kael being on my mind.

I stared at him, the words hitting me like a physical blow. "A ball? Is that really necessary?"

"It is," he said firmly. "This marriage is essential for Eldoria's future. You understand that don't you?"

I nodded slowly, though I was screaming inside my own head.

Essential? Fucking hell, why does my life have to be sacrificed for the kingdom? What about what I want? What about... Kael's image flashed in my mind again, and Bethany's words came unbidden. *"You looked like his little harlot."*

A small, defiant voice inside me answered: *"Yes... For Kael, I'll be his little harlot. If that's what he wants, I'd gladly give it to him."*

I couldn't help but slip a smile thinking about it. I simply curtsied, hiding the turmoil roiling within me, and left the throne room.

Standing on the castle balcony, I stared out over the snowy expanse of Eldoria. The wind bit at my cheeks, but I barely felt it. My mind was consumed with Kael... his accusations of corruption, his touch, and the impossible pull I felt toward him.

For better or worse, my life was no longer my own. But I would find a way to navigate this storm. For my kingdom. For myself. And, though I couldn't admit it aloud, for Kael. But I had to see him again....

CHAPTER XI
REBEL DESIRE

I was born into a gilded cage. It was lined with velvet, laced with gold, built on centuries of power and conquest. I was raised to be a queen, molded by duty, forged by expectation. My fate was written before I even took my first breath. But I have never been the kind of woman to let anyone decide my fate for me. The first lesson they teach a princess is obedience. We are told we must be graceful, we must be wise, we must be worthy of the crown that will one day sit upon our heads. We are taught how to smile while swallowing bitterness, how to curtsey while the chains tighten around our throats. But no one teaches us how to fight. No one teaches us what to do when the walls start to close in, when the weight of expectation is too heavy to bear, when our own heart begins to betray us.

I should have been prepared. I should have known. Because the moment I locked eyes with him, the moment I stepped into his storm, everything changed. Kael. The name alone was a curse, a whispered warning spoken in the halls of Eldoria. A barbarian. A monster. A man who bathed in war and wore death like a second skin. The stories about him were meant to make children fear the dark, to remind nobles of their place, to keep the kingdom's borders standing strong. But I have always been drawn to the dark. And when I stood before him, when his icy blue gaze pinned me in place, when his presence wrapped around me like a predator deciding whether to devour its prey, I felt something I had never felt before. Not fear. Freedom. It wasn't supposed to be this way.

I came here for duty. For my people. For peace. I was meant to sit across from him, to negotiate, to forge a future that would keep my kingdom safe. But the fire in his eyes set something ablaze inside me that I did not know existed. And the moment his hand wrapped around my wrist, the moment his voice rumbled through my very bones, I knew I would never be the same. I was raised to see men like him as beasts. Uncivilized. Unworthy. Beneath me. But how do you call something a beast when it looks at you like it sees the deepest parts of your soul? How do you call something unworthy when it makes you feel more alive than you have ever been? How do you call something beneath you when it stands like a king, like a god, like something forged from war itself?

I should have walked away. I should have turned my back and never looked back. But when you have spent your life in a cage, even a wildfire looks like salvation. And Kael? He was the kind of wildfire that would burn me alive. But I would go willingly. I would go smiling. Because for the first time in my life... I wasn't afraid of the flames.

CHAPTER XII

BEYOND THE EDGE OF REASON

KAEL

T he night was still, save for the low crackle of the fire burning at the center of my tent. Shadows danced across the canvas walls, flickering shapes a reflection of the thoughts swirling in my mind. My gaze flicked to the war map spread before me, but for once, I found myself unable to focus. The image of Seraphina lingered, her defiance, her composure, and that hint of vulnerability that seeped through despite her best efforts. A sound outside broke my reverie, the faint unmistakable rhythm of hooves crunching through snow.

"Alistair," I said, my voice low but commanding. Without a word, he rose from his place near the tent's edge and stepped outside to investigate. I stayed seated, listening intently.

"Identify yourself!" Alistair's voice rang out, sharp and firm. There was a pause, then the faint murmur of a woman's voice. I stood; curiosity piqued and pulled the tent flap aside just enough to peer out. My eyes landed on the cloaked figure atop the horse, her hood concealing her face. Alistair's sword gleamed in the moonlight as he approached, wary. "Reveal yourself," he ordered. The figure reached up, pulling back the hood, and my breath caught in my chest. Seraphina.

What the fuck was she doing here? Alone, no guards, no entourage. Just her. Alistar glanced back at me, his expression questioning. I gave him a curt nod, motioning for him to let her through. He sheathed his sword, then helped her down from the horse.

"Will he see me?" she asked softly, her voice carrying a strange mix of hesitation and determination. Alistair didn't answer, just gestured toward the tent. As she approached, I stepped back inside, letting the flap fall closed. She entered cautiously, her pale blue cloak dusted with snow, the fur lining framing her face like a halo. The firelight caught in her hair, casting a warm glow over her features. She didn't speak at first, just stood there, fidgeting slightly.

"What is the nature of your business here?" I asked, my tone sharp. "There are no guards, nobody accompanies you. Can I take it that my terms were rejected?" Her lips parted, but no sound came out. She seemed... Unsure, a stark contrast to the composed princess I had met before. "Speak, girl," I pressed, leaning back in my seat. She swallowed, closing her mouth before attempting again.

"I may seem like... I'm fucking crazy. Please excuse my language..."

I cut her off with a wave of my hand. "Princess, I don't give a damn how you speak here. Now, why have you come in the dead of night, back to my tent of all places?" Her silence stretched, her nervous energy palpable. I watched as she fidgeted, her hands clasping and unclasping at her sides. She finally took a deep breath, then stepped forward, kneeling before me.

"Gods forgive me," she murmured, so softly I almost didn't hear it. She looked up at me, her eyes blazing with a fire that sent a shiver down my spine. "You were right about our interaction when I was here last. I fucking loved it." Her confession hung in the air, raw and unfiltered. I leaned forward, resting my elbows on my thighs as I studied her.

"You rode all this way, in the middle of the night, to tell me I was right?"

She straightened slightly, her chin lifting in defiance. "No, that's not the only reason I came. I can't stop fucking thinking about you. You're the only thing I can think of. It's like you've infected my goddamn brain." Her words were unguarded, desperate, and they seemed to stir something deep within me.

SERAPHINA

His eyes bore into me, unyielding and unreadable. My heart thundered in my chest as I forced the words out, each one a piece of the dam breaking inside me.

"You've infected my brain." I said again, my voice trembling. "I am supposed to be betrothed to another, in service of my kingdom. I've never been with a man, and until I met you, the thought terrified me. But now..." I paused, trying to gather my thoughts, but it was fucking useless. Every fiber of my being was drawn to him, and my words spilled out before I could stop them. I didn't want to stop them. I needed him to know how I felt. "Now, you're all I can think about. That day in this very tent, if you'd wanted me... You could have had me. You could have fucked me right there, and I would have let you." The admission burned my cheeks, but I couldn't stop. "No matter what you did to me, it only made me want you more. I need more. I need you." Kael leaned back in his throne, his gaze never leaving mine. The firelight played across his face, highlighting the sharp planes of his features. He was silent for a moment, his expression remained unreadable, and it made my pulse race.

"You rode all this way, in the dead of night, to tell me that?" He asked again, his voice low and dangerous.

"Yes," I whispered, my voice barely audible.

"Do you have any idea what you're saying, Princess?" His tone was sharp; a warning wrapped in curiosity.

"I know exactly what I'm saying," I replied, my voice steadying. "I don't care what it costs me. My Kingdom, my duty... None of it matters. I refuse to fight this anymore." Kael rose from his throne, towering over me. His presence was overwhelming, and I felt my breath hitch as he stepped closer.

"You would be mine, rather than lead your own kingdom?" he questioned. I saw this as my one and only opportunity to tell him exactly how I felt, so I let it out without thinking further...

"I would, I would be your princess. I would be your harlot to do with as you please, I fucking would. I am here now because *you* are MY KING." He stood there before me. He leaned down and grabbed me by my hair and gave me a passionate kiss. Our tongues were intertwined as if they were one. ***My GODS***, *it made me wet. It only made me want him more.* He stood back up and looked down on me.

"Princess," he said, his voice a growl, "you're playing a dangerous game." I looked up at him, my heart hammering against my ribs.

"Then let it burn." With that I couldn't stand it anymore. I reached out for his belt and tugged frantically at it trying to get it off of him. He placed his hands over mine and started helping me undo the buckle. As he did, with one swift motion, he pulled his belt off and wrapped it around my neck. He looped it through the buckle and pulled hard to tighten it up on my throat. I FUCKING LOVED IT! As it tightened on my throat,

I let out an uncontrollable moan. Kael kept the belt tight in his fist to keep tension on it. His dark brown trousers had started to slip down, and I needed them off. I reached up to help them slide down and as I did... Inch by inch his cock came into view. My mouth started watering instantly. As I slid his trousers down further... The head of his cock peeked out. With a stream of pre-cum dripping down... I fucking lost it. Almost instinctively, I opened my hungry mouth. I stuck my tongue out and began licking the head of his cock trying to taste all of him. His pre-cum was so sweet. I was so fucking wet my dress had now been soaked. I felt him let out a low groan... And it made me want more of him.

I felt him pulling at the belt as his cock started sliding deeper and deeper into my mouth. The more I sucked, the tighter the belt got around my throat. By now, his belt was so tight around my neck, I started to get light-headed... But I wasn't stopping. I wanted him. I needed him. Each time I pulled back, I was trying to shove as much of him as I could possibly get down my throat. Each time I shoved, I could feel myself start to gag... Tears started to well up in my eyes. I'm not sure if it was lack of air... Or if I was in so much bliss that I was starting to cry tears of joy. I didn't fucking care. I was his. Suddenly, he grabbed me by my hair and helped me to my feet. I was gasping for air, breathing so heavily I thought I may pass out. I could feel as I stood up my pussy was soaking wet, aching for attention. Kael reaches for a dagger he has laying on the bench beside us and holds it up in front of my face. I let out a long slow breath... Quivering with anticipation to see what he is going to do. He takes the dagger and puts it in between my breasts... And cuts straight down my dress. He throws the dagger to the ground and rips the rest of my dress off of me.

He picks me up in his arms like I was fucking nothing. He carries me over to his bed and crawls into it with me in his arms. He lays me down and I position myself for him... I was sooooo fucking ready. He crawls in-between my legs. I feel the warmth of his body on my skin. It felt so good. The light of the fire casting our shadows on the walls of his tent made it look as if we were doing some kind of erotic dance with each other. He meets my eyes and leans down to kiss me. As he kisses me, I feel his cock slowly guide its way inside me. In the midst of his kiss, I let out a deep gasp. Oh, My Gods! I could feel every inch of his cock as it stretched me. Every vein, he felt as if he was shooting thunderbolts all over my body! I look into his eyes and whisper, "Take me, my king." He lets out a loud groan as he slides further into me.

"Fuuuuccckkk." He moans. I wrap my arms around him as he starts thrusting into me. Every thrust sending shockwaves all over my body. I began moaning so loudly I could hardly catch my breath in between his powerful thrusts. My soul needed him so badly. My nails had started to dig into his now sweaty back. I could feel his muscles tense every time he thrust into me.

"Kael, take me!" I screamed out. My body had started to shake into convulsions. Every muscle in my body had started to tense up all at once. He started thrusting harder...... And faster...... And faster... And with a last loud moan, I felt him explode inside of me.

"AAaaahhhhh, FFuuuuccckkk!" He growled. The fire burned low, casting a warm glow over the tent. I lay there, my heart still racing, my body still trembling from the intensity of what had just transpired. Kael laid beside me, silent, as we both were trying to catch our breath. I wanted to speak, to say something... anything, but the weight of the moment held me in silence. Whatever had just happened, it had changed everything. Kael finally looked at me, his expression unreadable as usual. "You understand what this means, don't you?" I nodded, my voice barely above a whisper.

"Yes." He leaned over to me, his eyes narrowing as he studied me.

"Good. Because there's no turning back now, Princess."

His words hung heavy in the air, their implications sinking deep into my chest. I didn't know what the future held, but in that moment, I didn't fucking care. All that mattered was him.

And I knew, deep down, that I would follow him through the pits of hell.

CHAPTER XIII
THE GILDED CAGE

SERAPHINA

T he grand hall was suffocating. Glittering chandeliers hung overhead, their light glinting off polished silver trays and the embellished goblets clutched in noble hands. The scent of roasted meats and spiced wine hung thick in the air, but it turned my stomach. All I could think about was how false it all felt... the smiles, the congratulations, the cheers for a union I didn't want.

I stood at the center of the hall like a porcelain doll, draped in elegance, yet hollow inside. The corset of my gown was tighter than I liked, deep sapphire blue with silver embroidery, cinched so perfectly it felt more like a noose. I forced a delicate smile, bowing my head gracefully as noblewomen fawned over me.

I hate this. I fucking hate all of it.

The words seared in my mind as another woman clasped my hands, tears in her eyes as she congratulated me for my "good fortune."

Good fortune? To be handed to someone I didn't love like some gilded gift wrapped for convenience? Alaric stood beside me, beaming as if he'd won some grand prize. I was not *his* fucking prize. His arm brushed against mine, and I had to resist the urge to flinch.

*He thinks I'm **his**. What a fucking joke.*

I forced another polite nod as the music swelled, signaling the start of the formal announcement. My father rose from his seat at the head of the table, clearing his throat. His booming voice silenced the room, and all eyes turned toward us.

"Today, we celebrate the union that will secure our kingdom's future." His words were met with cheers and applause.

Alaric took my hand, raising it for all to see, and the applause swelled louder. My fingers felt cold in his grip. It made my skin crawl.

They're cheering for a lie.

I barely registered my father's speech. My gaze drifted over the crowd, the faces blurred as memories pulled me elsewhere. I saw Kael's eyes staring back at me from the firelight in his tent. I remembered the strength in his hands and the way his voice rumbled like thunder. The warmth that spread through me at the memory made me shiver.

My mind betrayed me, dragging me back to that night when I knelt in his presence, powerless yet utterly willing. I remembered the way he had looked at me, not as a princess, not as a prize, but as a woman he could take apart piece by piece until I was nothing but his. I *am* his. He made me his.

Gods help me. I fought to control my breathing, but my heart hammered in my chest. Heat pooled low in my stomach, and I cursed myself for how easily his memory unraveled me. Just the thought of Kael made me wet.

Alaric pulled me onto the dance floor for the first waltz, his smile wide and sure. The music played, sweet and elegant, but I heard only static.

He spun me gracefully, but all I could think was how I wished it was Kael's arms holding me instead. Kael didn't move with elegance, he moved with raw, unrefined power.

Fuck. Stop it, Seraphina.

Alaric's hand pressed gently against my lower back. He leaned in slightly. "You look breathtaking tonight," he murmured, his voice low.

I forced a tight-lipped smile. "You're too kind."

I'd rather be anywhere but here.

The scent of wine clung to his breath. He smiled again, blissfully unaware that I was standing here, dreaming of another man. Dreaming of Kael's rough hands and his voice rumbling in my ear like a storm. Kael, *My* King who I had given myself to, just days ago.

The dance ended, and the guests erupted into applause. I curtsied with perfect poise, though every muscle in my body screamed to flee.

As the night dragged on, the guests came forward to offer their blessings and congratulations. Alaric basked in it all, shaking hands and nodding as if he were already a king. I rolled my eyes hoping no one had seen.

There was no fucking way I was marrying this man.

My responses were automatic... smiles, curtsies, soft words of gratitude. But inside, I felt like screaming. The ball was finally winding down. People began to drift out, the music quieted, and the last of the nobles offered their final goodbyes.

The moment the last guest was gone, I exhaled and allowed the tight mask of composure to slip for just a second. I turned on my heel and made my way to my chambers.

The warmth of the fire greeted me as I entered my room, but it didn't soothe me. I moved to the corner and began unfastening the intricate laces of my gown, shedding the heavy fabric and replacing it with simple riding clothes.

As I pulled on my boots, Bethany entered without knocking.

"Seraphina." Her voice was soft but wary. "You're going out again, aren't you?"

I didn't look at her. "Yes."

Bethany sighed, closing the door behind her. "Do you have any idea how reckless this is? Someone will notice. Alaric is already watching you like a hawk."

I turned to face her, tying the leather cords at my waist. "I don't care."

Bethany crossed her arms. "You should."

I took a deep breath, choosing my words carefully. "Bethany, I haven't been honest with you." I hesitated, but the truth bubbled up like a confession. "The last time I saw Kael... I gave myself to him."

Bethany's eyes widened. "You mean..."

"Yes." I held her gaze steadily. "I've chosen my king, Bethany. And it's not Alaric."

Bethany's face softened, but there was still a flicker of fear in her eyes. "I understand, but... Seraphina, are you willing to die for him?"

I smiled, a slow, defiant grin. "No, Bethany. I intend to live for him."

Bethany stared at me in silence, then nodded. "I'll cover for you. Just... Be careful."

I crossed to the window, pulling it open and staring out at the snow-covered night. The wind bit at my face, but I didn't care.

"Thank you, my dearest friend," I whispered before swinging my legs over the ledge.

As I climbed down into the night, the cold air filled my lungs, but my heart was on fire. As my boots landed on the ground, a couple castle maids were passing by. I had hoped they hadn't seen me, but no such luck.

"Princess?" one of the maids called out. "What on earth are you doing out here at this time of night? You should get back inside, you'll catch cold."

I flipped up the hood from my cloak and I said "I'm just going for a late-night ride is all. I'll be sure to be careful."

"M'Lady, you should be bringing a few knights with you for protection, you never know what you'll run into out here." the other maid said with a bit of skepticism on her breath.

"I don't think that necessary. I'm sure I won't run into any trouble." I assured her.

"Would you like me to inform Lord Alaric, Malakar, or perhaps your father just in case M'Lady?" the first one asked with a smirk on her face.

"NO!" I blurted out. "Do not do that. It's not needed. I won't be long. Just getting some air." I lied.

"Ok miss, well, you be careful." They said as they both walked off, side-eying me. *I sure hope that doesn't come back to bite me in the ass.*

I was no longer a pawn on someone else's board. I was no longer a prisoner in a gilded cage. I was something more... something wild, unbroken. And I was riding straight toward the man who had shown me who I really was.

CHAPTER XIV
THE SHADOWS OF FATE

Kael

The fire burned low in the center of the tent, the embers crackling softly as I stared at the map spread before me. The lines of Eldoria's borders blurred together as my thoughts wandered. My hand drifted to the hilt of my sword, resting there out of habit. The weight of decisions, the weight of her, pressed on my chest like a goddamned boulder.

Seraphina.

No matter how hard I tried; I couldn't get her out of my head. She'd infected me like a curse; one I didn't want to break. The way she looked at me, her eyes seared into my mind, her body trembling with a mixture of fear and desire... It made me feel like a man who could tear the gods themselves down from the heavens. The tent was quiet, too quiet. Outside, the cold wind hissed through the camp, but in here, the silence was suffocating. I leaned forward, gripping the edges of the table.

"I know you're there," I muttered, my voice low. The shadows in the corner shifted, and there she was.

Elysandra.

"Still as sharp as ever, my boy," she said, stepping into the fire-light. Her red hair shimmered like molten copper, and her green eyes sparkled with that knowing glint that always unsettled me. I exhaled, leaning back in my chair.

"You could at least announce yourself for once."

"And miss the chance to see you squirm? Never." She smiled, that sly curve of her lips both infuriating and oddly comforting. I studied her as she moved closer, draping herself onto the bench across from me with the grace of a predator at rest.

"What do you want, Elysandra?" Her expression softened, and for the first time in a long while, I saw something deeper behind her usual playfulness.

"To talk." I crossed my arms, watching her closely.

"Talk about what?" She leaned forward, her green eyes steady on mine.

"About the past. About where this path you are currently on is leading you." My jaw tightened.

"I know where I'm going."

"Do you? Do you think it mere happenstance that you and your newfound obsession... can't stop thinking of one another? Do you truly believe that its divine affinity... or fate perhaps?" she asked, her voice soft but pointed. The fire crackled between us, and I felt the memories clawing their way back to the surface. I clenched my fists, trying to shove them down, but her gaze pinned me in place. "You've also carried that night with you for years," she said. "The fire, the screams, your father's voice. You think I don't know that it still haunts you?" I looked up sharply, anger flaring in my chest.

"I should have known you had something to do with all this" She sighed, brushing a strand of hair from her face.

"Kael, I was there. I found you under my tree stump, remember? I saw the smoke, smelled the ash. I carried you to Morvath with my own hands. And as for your beloved... that was always going to happen. One way or the other." The memory hit me like a punch to the gut. Her voice, soft and soothing, came rushing back to me. *You're safe now.*

"You saved me." I said, the words feeling foreign in my mouth.

"I did," she replied, her tone steady. "Because I knew what you could become. I knew you were meant for more than dying on a farm in Eldoria's shadow. And I also knew you'd meet her, I knew who she was... who she was destined to be... and I know your role in the whole ball of wax." My fists unclenched, but the anger didn't fade entirely.

"And for what? So, I could become a man who kills for power? Who leads an army into blood and fire? To become a man who falls in love with his enemy?" Elysandra shook her head.

"No, Kael. So, you could survive. So, you could build something better. And don't tell me you haven't, those men out there follow you not because of fear, but because you give them hope. And your beloved... the touch of a woman. A woman will help a great man become greater. He will do things for her, he never dreamed of doing." Her voice lowered, taking on that eerie calm that always unsettled me. "But now, you stand at a crossroads. The hardest battles you've ever faced are still ahead of you." I scowled.

"I've fought my whole life. What's a couple more?" She tilted her head, her expression growing sad.

"It's not just a couple more, Kael. If you continue down this path... You will meet your fate." My chest tightened.

"What fate?" Her gaze didn't waver. "A fate where someone else will stand as Seraphina's king. Someone else will wear the crown you've fought for. And a child with your fire will be born, Kael... a daughter... but you'll never see her grow up." The words hit like a hammer to my chest. My breathing quickened as the weight of what she was saying sank in.

"No," I growled, shaking my head. "That's not happening. I won't let it happen." Elysandra's eyes softened. "Fate doesn't care about your will, Kael. It only cares about balance. If you love her... truly love her—then you need to be ready to face what comes."

The tent flap rustled, and Alistair stepped inside. His eyes immediately went to Elysandra, narrowing."

You again," he muttered, his hand resting on the hilt of his sword. Elysandra smirked, leaning back against the bench.

"You always say that as if I'm not welcome."

"You always show up when things are about to go to shit," Alistair said bluntly. She laughed softly, standing and stepping toward him.

"Maybe I'm here to keep you alive, Alistair. Ever think of that?" His jaw tightened, but he didn't move as she approached. Her eyes glimmered with playful mischief as she leaned closer. "If I wanted to, I could have you wrapped around my finger in seconds." Alistair's face reddened slightly, and he scowled.

"You can try." Elysandra chuckled, brushing past him toward the exit. She paused at the tent flap, turning back to me. The playfulness was gone, replaced by something somber and resolute. "You've come too far to falter now, Kael," she said. "But you need to be ready for what's coming. The storm is closer than you think." I met her gaze, the weight of her words pressing down on me like iron.

"I won't let it take her from me." Elysandra's lips curved into a sad smile.

"Then fight, Kael. Fight like hell. But remember... Not every battle can be won." And with that, she disappeared into the night, leaving the scent of wildflowers and ash in her wake. I stood there for a long moment, staring at the tent flap. Her words echoed in my mind like the tolling of a bell: *Someone else will wear the crown. A child with your fire will be born. And you'll never see her grow up.* I clenched my fists, my jaw tightening.

"Fate be damned," I growled. "If it thinks it can take her from me, it has no idea what kind of fight it's in for." The fire crackled softly as I turned back to the map, resolve hardening in my chest. Let the storm come.

CHAPTER XV
FLAME OF DESIRE

SERAPHINA

The wind bit at my cheeks as I rode through the dark forest, my hood pulled tight around my face. My breath fogged the cold night air, mingling with the sound of my horse's hooves crunching against the snow-covered ground. The icy chill seeped through my riding cloak, its pale blue fabric lined with fur, but even the cold couldn't extinguish the fire burning within me.

Kael.

His name echoed in my mind with every hoof beat, a constant rhythm that matched the pounding of my heart. I needed to see him, to feel his presence again. The memory of his touch, his voice, the way his eyes bore into mine... it consumed me.

The two-hour ride from Eldoria's castle to Kael's camp dragged on like an eternity. My body ached from the tension, my thighs gripping the saddle as my horse galloped through the darkness. I tried to focus on the path ahead, but my thoughts kept slipping back to him.

I barely noticed the figure at first. A flicker of red hair, illuminated by the moonlight, caught my eye among the trees. I jerked the reins, pulling my horse to a stop, my heart skipping a beat.

"Hello?" I called, my voice trembling slightly.

There was no response, only the soft rustle of the wind through the branches. I scanned the snow-covered ground for footprints, but there was nothing...no sign of anyone.

"Hello?" I tried again, louder this time, but the forest swallowed my words.

I chuckled nervously, shaking my head. "Fuck's sake, Seraphina. You're spooking yourself."

I urged my horse forward, the reins tight in my hands. The figure was gone, and I told myself it had been a trick of the moonlight. Still, unease prickled at my skin.

The glow of fires in the distance signaled Kael's camp, and relief flooded through me. As I approached, the outlines of men seated around one of the fires became clearer. My horse slowed to a trot, then stopped a few paces from the group. I dismounted, the snow crunching beneath my boots.

Alistair rose from his seat, his hand resting on the hilt of his sword. His face softened when he recognized me.

"Princess Seraphina," he said, his voice low but respectful. "What brings you here at this hour?"

Before I could answer, one of the men to his left sneered.

"I can't believe this fucking wench is here," the man muttered, loud enough for everyone to hear. "It's her goddamn fault we're out here freezing our asses off."

I froze, my stomach twisting in anger and embarrassment.

Alistair turned on him instantly. "Shut your fucking mouth, or I'll shut it for you."

The man ignored him, gesturing toward me with a dismissive wave. "We're risking our lives for this bitch, and she's cozying up to our king like some..."

He didn't finish his sentence.

The sound of boots crunching on snow cut through the man's rant. I turned my head, and there he was... Kael, stepping out of his tent, his silhouette framed by the firelight. His dark eyes scanned the scene, taking in the tension, the agitation in the air.

The man didn't notice Kael's approach, too absorbed in his tirade.

"She's nothing but trouble, and now she's..."

Kael grabbed the man's hair, yanking his head back so hard I heard the crack of his neck snapping into position. The man's eyes went wide, his bravado crumbling into sheer terror.

Kael leaned down, his voice low and cold. "So, you enjoy talking, do you?"

The man stammered, his words fumbling out in a pathetic attempt at an apology. "M'Lord, I... I didn't mean nuffin' by it..."

Kael straightened, his gaze sweeping over the group. The other men sat frozen, their faces pale, while Alistair watched with a grim expression. When Kael's eyes met mine, my breath caught.

"My Queen," he said, his voice a quiet growl. "You don't want to know what happens next."

Oh, gods. He called me his queen. My knees went weak, my body betraying me as heat pooled deep within me. I tried to keep my composure, but the way he looked at me, like I belonged to him... made me feel as if I would shatter.

I looked upon the man, a wave rushed over me. I peered into the blackness of his eyes. I felt nothing. I then looked up at Kael, into his deep blue eyes.

"Show me, My King," I said softly, my voice trembling with a mix of fear and desire.

His lips curled into a slow, wicked grin. "As you wish."

Kael shoved the man forward, forcing him onto his knees. He grabbed the back of his head and drove his face into the flames of the fire.

The man's screams pierced the night, a horrifying symphony of pain and desperation. The smell of burning flesh filled the air, mingling with the putrid stench of singed hair. The other men looked away, their faces pale, but I couldn't. I couldn't stop watching.

Kael held the man there, his expression unchanging, his strength unwavering. When he finally pulled the man's head from the flames, his face was unrecognizable... blackened, blistered, and wet with tears and saliva.

"Are you hungry?" Kael asked, his voice calm, almost mocking.

The man whimpered, his words incoherent.

Kael tilted his head, then looked at me. His grin returned, darker this time. "My Queen, he seems to enjoy talking. Should we feed him?"

My heart raced, my body trembling as I nodded, unable to form words.

Kael unsheathed his dagger and grabbed the man's jaw. "Open your mouth," he ordered.

The man obeyed, his sobs wracking his body.

In one swift motion, Kael cut out the man's tongue. Blood sprayed across the snow, and the man howled, his cries muffled by the torrent of red spilling from his mouth.

Kael held the severed tongue over the fire, letting it char before shoving it back into the man's mouth. "Chew it," he commanded.

The man obeyed; his agony written in every jerky motion of his jaw.

Kael leaned down, his dagger pressing against the man's teeth. "If you survive this, you'll never utter another word. If you do, I'll carve you into pieces and leave you for the wolves."

With a sharp motion, Kael slammed his knee into the man's jaw, shattering his teeth. Blood spilled onto the snow as the man crumpled to the ground.

Kael straightened, his dark eyes meeting mine. He extended his bloodied dagger toward me.

Without thinking, I reached out, my fingers curling around his wrist. I leaned forward, my tongue brushing the blade, tasting the blood.

Kael's grin widened, and he pulled me to my feet. "Come with me, My Queen."

And I followed him, my heart racing, my body burning, knowing I would follow him into the depths of hell if he asked.

Kael's hand wrapped around my wrist, pulling me away from the campfire. My heart hammered in my chest, and my legs felt weak, but I followed him without hesitation. The camp faded into the distance as we moved into the forest. The snow crunched softly beneath our boots, the only sound in the still, icy night.

The moon was impossibly bright, hanging in the sky like a glowing beacon. Its light bathed the clearing we entered, making the snow shimmer like it was dusted with diamonds. It was breathtaking, the kind of scene you'd think existed only in stories.

Our footsteps trailed behind us, the only marks in the untouched snow. The cold bit at my cheeks, but it didn't matter. Nothing mattered except him.

Kael stopped in the center of the clearing; his broad shoulders outlined by the moonlight. His presence felt like a shield against the cold, against everything.

"I shouldn't have come," I blurted out, my words tumbling over each other as they spilled from my lips. "I mean, it's the middle of the night, and I know you have your men to lead and a war to fight, and I... I couldn't help it, Kael. I can't stop thinking about you. You're in my head constantly. It's like you've taken over my mind, and I... fuck, I needed to see you. I couldn't stay away. It's like..."

"My Queen."

His voice was calm, steady, a stark contrast to my breathless rambling. He raised a single finger to my lips, silencing me with a simple touch.

My heart nearly stopped.

"Quiet your mind," he said softly, his breath forming thick clouds in the frigid air. "Listen."

I blinked up at him, my thoughts scattering like the snowflakes drifting around us. He wrapped his arms around me and pulled me close resting my head upon his chest.

"What do you hear?" he asked, his voice a low rumble that sent a shiver down my spine.

I paused, closing my eyes for a moment. The wind whispered through the trees, and the silence of the forest enveloped us. But none of that mattered. I opened my eyes, locking onto his.

"I hear your heart," I whispered.

His lips curled into a soft smile, and he lifted his hand to cup my cheek. His palm was warm, calloused, grounding me in a way nothing else could. I placed my hand over his, my fingers curling around his as if to hold onto this moment forever.

He leaned down, and his lips captured mine in a kiss that stole the breath from my lungs. It was deep, consuming, filled with everything words could never express.

When he pulled back, his forehead rested against mine, and his voice was a low murmur. "My heart beats for you now. It belongs to you."

Tears pricked at my eyes, but I didn't dare blink them away.

He straightened slightly, his hand never leaving my cheek. "Look at the moon," he said, his tone soft but commanding.

I tilted my head back, my gaze lifting to the glowing orb in the sky.

"As long as that moon is in the sky at night, I will be with you," he said. "All you need to do is look up and know I am looking at the same moon, underneath the same sky."

As he said those words, I needed him. Fuck I needed him. I needed him inside me once more. I held my hands up to my mouth and breathed into them to warm them up. Then I took both of them and stuck them down the front of his trousers and started rubbing my hands on his cock.

"My Queen, here in the snow?" He whispered to me.

I looked into his eyes as I was rubbing his cock. I could feel it becoming rigid in my hands. Fuck I loved how it felt.

"Yes, My King, you can have me anywhere. I need you. I need to feel you inside me."

He leaned down to kiss me as my breathing started to become heavier the more I thought about him.

"Lay down in the snow, My King, please allow me to love you." I begged.

He looked around for a second and then laid down in the diamond-sparkled snow. I lifted my dress, and I straddled him as he lay in the snow. My knees planted firmly into the snow on each side of him. I reached up under my dress that had been draped over him to feel for his cock. I leaned forward to kiss him as I fumbled with his trousers to take his cock out and started rubbing it against my pussy.

"Uuuuhhhhh!" I moaned uncontrollably as his cock touched me.

I took a deep breath, and I slid his cock slowly inside of me. I let out another moan as he slid inside of me. Fuck it was satisfying for me to have him. I placed both of my hands upon his chest to steady myself. I could feel the icy snow on my knees. It felt like daggers piercing my skin. There was no amount of discomfort or pain I would not endure for him.

Fuck, he felt like sin carved into flesh, every touch; a brand searing itself into me. I moaned again as I leaned back all the way down on his cock. My body heat rose so much that steam was radiating off of me as I grinded myself into him. I felt Kael's hands wrap around and he placed each of his hands on each of my ass cheeks.

I felt him squeeze tightly to my ass as he started lifting me up and down, up and down.

Oh, my Gods, he felt like violence disguised as pleasure, tearing me apart and stitching me back together in the same breath! I started rocking my hips back and forth as if they had a mind of their own. My nails started to dig into his chest as my body started to shake.

"Uuuhhhhh!" I moaned quivering from bliss.

He moved his hands to my shoulders, his breathing short but heavy. Kael put pressure on my shoulders as if he was trying to put more of his cock inside of me.

"I... I'm... C-c-c-cum-ming, My King!" I moaned out.

My body tensed and shook as I felt my pussy tighten around Kael's cock.

"Aaahhh-aaahhhh" He groaned.

He shoved his cock as far inside me as he could, and I felt him explode.

Like I had just fought a goddamn war, every thrust a battle I never wanted to win. I collapsed onto Kael's chest. We laid there in the snow and cold in utter silence. Breathing heavily, fog from our breath rose into the air like thick smoke.

The moonlit clearing became our sanctuary, a world where only the two of us existed. As the snow continued to fall, I knew I would carry this moment with me forever, a secret carved into the depths of my soul. For the first time in my life, I felt whole. Kael pulled me close again, his arms wrapping around me as if he could shield me from the world. And for the first time, I needed him to.

CHAPTER XVI

THE HEART'S CONFESSION

Kael

The world outside the tent was frozen, snow still clung to the folds of the canvas, and the cold wind screamed its rage across the tundra like it knew what we'd done. But inside, the air was thick. Warm. Heavy with her scent and mine.

Seraphina lay beside me, her skin like fire pressed against mine, and for once, I let myself stop thinking. Just... breathe.

Her body molded against me as if it had always belonged there, her leg hooked over mine, her fingers still resting on my chest where they'd clawed during release. Her cheek was nestled near my shoulder, breath soft, uneven, like she was still coming down from wherever I'd taken her.

Gods, she was beautiful.

Not in the way that poems captured, or bards sang about.

She was *feral*. Divine. Like winter itself had taken form and decided to burn.

I turned toward her, slowly, letting my hand drift up her spine with the care of a man holding a sacred weapon. Her eyes met mine, half-lidded, flushed, pupils still blown wide, and for a moment, I forgot how to breathe.

She was *real*.

That's what killed me the most.

Because I'd told myself, again and again, that this couldn't happen. That we were enemies. That this was politics. Strategy. War.

But there was no strategy in the way my chest ached when she smiled at me. No war tactic in the way I memorized the sound of her laugh. Nothing tactical about the way my soul seemed to lurch every time she walked into a room.

"I'm never going to be the same," I said, voice barely above a whisper.

She blinked slowly, studying me with those eyes that always seemed to see too much. She didn't answer. Didn't have to. So, I went on, needing her to hear the rot and ruin she'd left in me.

"You came into my life like a fire in the middle of a blizzard. Do you know that?" I whispered, fingers trailing up into her hair. I combed my hand through the dark silk of it, wrapping a strand around my finger just to feel something stay.

"I had ice where my heart used to be. A kingdom on my shoulders. Blood on my hands I stopped trying to wash off years ago. And then you," I laughed under my breath, bitter and quiet. "You shattered everything I thought I knew. Every wall I spent my entire life building? You burned it down without even meaning to."

She reached up, brushing her fingertips along my jaw. I caught her hand in mine and kissed her palm.

"You ruined me, Seraphina," I murmured, pressing my forehead to hers. "And I think I want you to ruin me again. Every night. Every gods-damned day until there's nothing left of me but *you.*"

Her breath caught. And in that second, I saw her tremble. Just slightly. Like I'd cracked something in her, too.

"I love you," I said, no hesitation. No armor. Just truth. Raw and violent and terrifying in its honesty. "I'm not saying it because it's expected. I'm saying it because it's the only thing I've ever been sure of. I love you like it's war. Like it's survival."

She moved to say something, but I touched her lips, silencing her.

"Let me finish. Just this once, let me say everything I've never said to anyone."

Her eyes searched mine, still guarded, still that sharp, calculating heir beneath the softness. But she nodded.

"You are the reason I stopped praying for peace and started praying for time. Time to have you. To know you. To keep you." I drew my thumb over her cheekbone, memorizing every line of her face like scripture. "I never believed in fate until you looked at me like I wasn't a monster."

Her expression shifted, somewhere between wonder and grief.

"You looked at me like I was a man worth saving," I whispered. "Like I was worth *loving*. And no one's ever done that. Not even me."

I tucked a lock of hair behind her ear and leaned in, kissing her slow, no hunger, no desperation. Just need. Just reverence.

When I pulled back, I pressed our foreheads together again, like I couldn't get close enough without sinking into her.

"I would burn kingdoms for you, Seraphina," I breathed. "And if you asked, I'd build new ones from the ashes. I'd bleed. I'd kneel. I'd die."

Her eyes were glassy now, lips parted, but no words came. That was fine. She didn't need to say anything.

"I don't want peace if it doesn't have you in it," I said. "I don't want a throne. I don't want a legacy. I want *you*. Your rage. Your fire. Your madness. I want your love, even if it kills me."

I kissed the tip of her nose, her brow, the corner of her mouth, each one slower than the last. Like I was saying goodbye to every version of me that existed before her.

She rolled toward me, straddling my waist, her hands on either side of my face. Her lips hovered inches above mine.

"I'm not going anywhere," she whispered.

Gods help me... I believed her.

I didn't know how long this would last, how much blood would be spilled, how many sins would come back to collect.

But in that moment, naked and wrapped in her heat, with the cold clawing outside and war on the horizon...

I would have burned the world to keep her warm.

SERAPHINA

The cold bit at my cheeks like a punishment.

Each breath I drew was sharp with frost, the wind curling around me like a ghost that hadn't made peace with its death. The horse beneath me moved steadily, hooves crunching through snow, but my body... it wasn't really *here*. Not anymore.

It was still back in that gods-damned tent. Wrapped in him.

Kael.

His name haunted every beat of my heart.

I shouldn't have let it happen, not once, and *definitely* not again. And yet, here I was, riding back to the keep like a woman who hadn't just sold her soul for the way his voice trembled when he whispered that he loved me.

"I would burn kingdoms for you."

My fingers tightened around the reins.

He meant it. That was the worst part.

He *meant* it.

It wasn't strategy. It wasn't seduction or manipulation. It was pure, unscripted madness. And I... gods forgive me... I *wanted* that madness.

I wanted to be the thing that unraveled him. That brought him to his knees, not with sword or sorcery, but with the mere suggestion of my absence. I wanted to live inside his head, his chest, his every breath. I wanted him to *crave* me with the same desperation that now sank its claws into *me*.

I could still feel him. The press of his fingertips in my hair. The warmth of his palm cupping my cheek like I was some delicate thing instead of a monster with a crown on her back and blood on her hands.

Kael didn't see the monster. He saw *me.*

And that was dangerous.

Because now I couldn't stop replaying every second of that moment.

His voice, low and ragged, trembling from the weight of his confession.

His eyes... those sharp, burning things that softened only for me.

His kiss, not devouring like before, but reverent. Like I was something sacred.

I should've pushed him away. Told him to shut the hells up and stop saying things that made the world tilt beneath my feet. But instead... I let him. I let him speak. I let him see. I *wanted* him to.

And now?

Now I was fucking *ruined.*

I was sick with it. Addicted to the sound of my name on his lips. Obsessed with the way his hands knew my body like they'd always belonged there. Possessed by every look, every touch, every word.

This wasn't love.

This was rot and hunger and fire.

And I *welcomed* it.

He was mine now, whether he knew it or not. Whether the world approved or not. Whether the gods dared to interfere or not.

Kael had planted his heart in my hands and said, *"Do what you will."*

And oh, I would.

I would cradle it. Worship it. Consume it if I had to.

Because for the first time in my life, I wasn't just playing at power. I wasn't wearing the mask of a queen-to-be, a pawn on a board, a pretty little heir with teeth hidden behind smiles.

No.

I *felt* powerful.

Because if Kael... the King of Morvath, the Butcher of the North, could shatter like glass in my hands...

Then the world didn't stand a chance.

I could see the castle in the distance now. The stone towers rising above the trees like watching eyes, dark and judging. I straightened in my saddle and forced a breath past my lips.

They couldn't know. No one could know what passed between us beneath those furs. The way he whispered his love like it was a confession to the gods.

I would keep it. Hide it. Hoard it like a dragon with gold.

Because it was *mine*.

And if anyone tried to take it away from me—

If anyone *dared* to come between me and what we had...

I would drown the realm in ash.

Smiling all the while...

CHAPTER XVII

THE CROWN WITHOUT A KING

LORD ALARIC

T he halls of Castle Eldor welcomed me with the reverence I deserved. Servants and nobles alike paused to acknowledge my presence, as they should. My boots echoed through the marble corridors, each step a reminder of the power I was soon to claim. My engagement to Princess Seraphina was not merely a union of hearts... it was a strategic move, a consolidation of power. The Kingdom of Eldoria and my own kingdom, Varethia, would soon be bound by marriage, and I would stand as the force behind the throne.

The Eldorian King was a wise ruler, but he was aging, and with age came weakness. In time, it would be my vision that shaped these lands. I adjusted the deep red cuffs of my embroidered tunic, smirking as I passed a pair of court ladies who curtsied with lowered eyes. If I had the time, I might have entertained their admiration, but I had more important matters to attend to... namely, my bride-to-be. Seraphina was an elusive one. She had a habit of vanishing for hours, if not days, at a time. No doubt she was off brooding in some candlelit study or wandering the castle gardens, lost in thought as princesses often were. But now that we were engaged, it was time for her to learn what was expected of her.

I reached her chamber doors and pushed them open without knocking. Why should I? Soon, everything she owned... her title, her lands, her very future, would belong to me. The room was shrouded in darkness, an odd choice for someone with nothing to hide. Heavy drapes sealed out the morning sun, casting long shadows over the stone walls. The air smelled faintly of lavender, but there was something else... something heavier. The unmistakable scent of damp wool and cold air. My gaze flickered to the chair beside her bedside. A pile of discarded riding clothes lay draped over it, dusted with dried mud and moisture, possibly from the melted snow. Curious. I made my way to the window, tugging the thick drapery aside with a sharp pull. Sunlight poured in, illuminating the disheveled sheets of the bed where Seraphina lay curled up, her dark hair tangled against the pillow.

She stirred, groaning slightly as the light struck her face. Slowly, those striking green eyes fluttered open, first squinting against the brightness, then locking onto me with thinly veiled irritation.

"Good morning, my dear," I said smoothly, perching on the edge of her bed with all the grace of a man who belonged there. Seraphina tensed, shifting beneath the covers.

"Lord Alaric." Her voice was polite, but I noted the restrained exasperation laced beneath it. I reached forward and brushed a stray strand of hair from her face. She flinched, so subtly it might have gone unnoticed by anyone else. Anyone but me.

"You're difficult to find, my dear. I must admit, it's quite a feat for a future queen to be so... Absent." I gestured toward the riding clothes in the chair. "You've been busy, I see." She glanced at them, her face an unreadable mask.

"An early morning ride. I find the fresh air clears the mind." I smiled.

"Ah, then perhaps I should accompany you sometime. I do believe it's important that we spend more time together, don't you? We *are* engaged, after all." Seraphina's lips parted as if she were about to protest, but I didn't allow her the opportunity. "In fact, I've taken the liberty of arranging several activities for us in the coming days. Hunting, for one. I'd love to show you how a true hunter takes down a stag." I leaned closer. "I'll even let you hold the bow, if you'd like." She blinked at me, her expression unreadable. "We'll also attend a dinner with the

Varethian nobles in two nights' time. And, of course, I have plans for an afternoon ride, followed by an evening of chess." I smirked. "Though I warn you, I rarely lose." Seraphina's posture remained rigid.

"That all sounds... Delightful." I studied her carefully. There was something about her that felt different, something in the way she held herself. It was almost as if she were... Tired. But of what? "Seraphina," I said, lowering my voice, "I know this arrangement is not the one you may have dreamed of as a child. But let us not forget, this marriage is bigger than the both of us. It is for the kingdom." She remained silent. "You *are* the future queen, and we must set an example. It would be unwise for the people to see you acting... Uninvested in our union." She stiffened slightly. I smiled, feigning concern. "What would the commoners think?" A muscle in her jaw twitched.

"Indeed." Satisfied, I patted her hand as if she were a child. "That's the spirit." The door creaked open and Seraphina's handmaiden, Bethany, entered the room, her eyes immediately darting between me and Seraphina with visible unease.

"M'Lord," she greeted stiffly, bowing her head.

"Ah, Bethany. Perfect timing," I said, standing from the bed. "Ensure that Seraphina is prepared for our outing tomorrow." Bethany shot Seraphina a wary glance.

"Of course, M'Lord." I took Seraphina's hand in mine, bringing it to my lips with a practiced kiss.

"Until tomorrow, my dear. Don't miss me too much." I turned on my heel and strode toward the door, my mind already elsewhere. The pieces were falling into place. Soon, everything I desired would be mine. And Seraphina? She would learn her place soon enough.

Leaving Seraphina's chambers, I made my way to the royal study where the King awaited. The guards outside his door recognized me instantly, stepping aside without question. Power had a way of parting crowds. Inside, the King sat behind a massive oak desk, aged but formidable, much like the man himself. By his side, as always, stood Malakar... the ever-watchful advisor, his presence like a shadow stitched to the throne.

"Ah, Lord Alaric," the King greeted, motioning me forward. "To what do I owe the pleasure this morning?" I inclined my head in respect.

"Your Majesty, I wished to discuss the progression of the engagement and the future of Eldoria." Malakar's eyes flicked to me, sharp and calculating. There was something unnerving about the man, as if he saw more than he let on. "The union is of great importance," I continued, "not just for us, but for the stability of the realm. I believe it's time we considered the next steps... arranging a date for the ceremony, securing alliances, and discussing the transition of certain responsibilities." The King nodded thoughtfully, but it was Malakar who spoke next.

"Indeed, the marriage will fortify Eldoria's standing. However, we must tread carefully. Change, even one as beneficial as this, can stir... Unrest." His voice was like silk wrapped around steel. I studied him, noting the way his words influenced the King's demeanor. There was a darkness there, subtle but pervasive. Malakar was more than an advisor... he was a puppeteer, his strings woven deep into the fabric of Eldoria's court.

"Unrest can be managed," I replied smoothly. "With strong leadership, the people will follow." Malakar's smile didn't reach his eyes.

"Leadership, yes. But power often lies not in the throne itself, but in the counsel that shapes it." *Is that so?* I thought, but I held my tongue. As the conversation continued, it became clear that Malakar's influence was far-reaching. He spoke of the kingdom's needs, the nobility's loyalty, and the importance of control, all framed as advice, but carrying the weight of command. The King listened intently, nodding along to Malakar's words, his own authority quietly eroded beneath layers of carefully crafted suggestions. *This man holds more power than he admits.* But power could be claimed. Malakar might pull the strings now, but soon enough, I would be the one holding the threads.

Marrying Seraphina was merely the first step. The real prize was Eldoria itself. As I left the study, I couldn't shake the feeling that Malakar was watching me, not as an ally, but as a rival. His smile lingered in my mind, a serpent coiled in the shadows, waiting. *Let him watch,* I thought. *He'll see soon enough who truly controls this kingdom.* I walked the corridors of Eldor with renewed purpose, my mind racing with plans and possibilities. Seraphina might resist, but she would fall in line. The King might trust his advisor, but trust was a fragile thing, easily shattered. And Malakar? He was a shadow. But even shadows vanish in the light.

CHAPTER XVIII
THE WITCH'S HOUR

ELYSANDRA

T he witch's hour is not marked by time... yet.

It is not struck by bells nor whispered by clocks. It bleeds into the world like something wounded, slow and sacred, drawn through the cracks in the veil by those of us foolish enough to touch what should not be touched.

The trees know me here. Their bark splits in reverence. Their roots curl inward, avoiding my steps. The moss glows faintly beneath my bare feet, aware of what I am, of what I carry. I step into the clearing, where the stone ruins of a temple older than kingdoms rise like broken teeth from the earth. The altar still holds the stain of gods long dead, and the air smells like copper, smoke, and memory.

My sanctuary.

My stage.

I draw the blade across my palm... an elegant, practiced cut. Blood wells instantly, rich and dark, eager. It drips from my fingers in slow, deliberate arcs, tracing the spiral of runes I've etched into the black stone.

Tonight, I am not a woman. I am a weaver. A warper of threads. A sovereign of consequence.

But just as I lower my hand to begin the ritual, the silence, divine, perfect... is shattered.

"Hey! Smells like someone's cooking up a fresh batch of trauma stew out here."

I don't even flinch. The voice is shrill, nasal, and unmistakably demonic.

Nibbles.

I don't turn around. I don't have to. He always appears the same way... like a fart in the middle of a sermon. Undignified. Loud. Unrepentant.

A flicker of movement darts above the altar. Something with a twitchy tail and no shame.

He crash-lands on one of the archways above, claws scrabbling gracelessly before he slides down a crumbling pillar with a dramatic, "Weeeeeee!" and lands ass-first in the blood circle I just drew.

Of course he does.

"Perfect," I mutter. "Just what my ritual needed. Ass grease and idiocy."

He blinks up at me, grinning like the unholy little troll he is. His face is a chaotic mix of raccoon and demon, too many teeth in the wrong places, glowing eyes that don't match, a snout that twitches like he's always smelling something foul... usually himself.

And gods help me... I summoned him.

It wasn't intentional, not really. Five centuries ago, during a binding ritual meant to call forth a familiar of immense magical power... preferably something regal and quiet... I mispronounced *one* syllable while bleeding over the seventh sigil. One.

Instead of a silent raven or a shadow-cat, I got *him*.

He crawled out of the summoning circle wearing a half-burned loincloth, singing a lewd tavern song and chewing on a moldy human foot.

And the worst part?

The bond *stuck*.

Magically tethered. Soul-locked. Eternal pain-in-my-ass status: permanent.

"Nice runes," Nibbles says, licking one. "Tastes like chicken blood and unprocessed mommy issues."

"That's because I used chicken blood," I say flatly. "And I *am* someone's mommy issue."

I return to the ritual. The runes hiss beneath my palm as I press blood into the ancient pattern, weaving magic into the air like threads through a loom. The forest groans in reply. Spirits shiver awake. Power answers me.

Nibbles scratches himself audibly and belches.

"Hey! Do you want to see my balls?" he asks

"I've seen them, they aren't that impressive." I answer.

"You know," he says, lounging on his back with his legs spread wide, tail twitching, "this whole 'fate-weaving' thing would be way more fun if you'd let me draw a dick in the middle."

"You *did* that last time," I snap, not looking up. "It altered the course of a noble bloodline and triggered a forty-year war."

"Best war ever," he sighs, dreamily. "So much screaming. So much incest."

"Honestly, if I ever figure out how to banish you..."

"You'll cry yourself to sleep without me. Admit it." He picks at something between his toes and flicks it at one of my candles. It extinguishes with a hiss.

I close my eyes. Inhale. Count to five. Exhale through clenched teeth.

"Why are you even here?" I ask, voice low and dangerous.

Nibbles shrugs. "Felt a tingle in my nipple. Knew you were up to something juicy."

"I'm always up to something juicy. I'm a witch, Nibbles. It's literally in the job description."

He climbs atop the altar now, crouching like a gargoyle mid-seizure. He coughs once, stirring ash and loose petals from the dried blooms I keep in bowls around the stones.

"I'm here for the show," he grins. "You're fate-weaving again, which means someone's about to get raw-dogged by destiny. Lemme guess... Seraphina and Captain Stoic-cock?"

I pause.

A slow smile tugs at my lips.

He's not wrong.

"They've crossed the threshold," I murmur. "He's given himself to her. Mind, body, soul."

Nibbles fans himself with a rotted leaf. "How *romantic*. Bet he whispered sweet nothings like, 'My trauma recognizes your trauma.'"

My smile widens. "He said he loved her."

"Ooooooooh, the '*L*' word! Dangerous game."

"He meant it." My voice darkens. "And she loves him."

Nibbles' eyes gleam. "Oh, you kinky puppet master. You *planned* this, didn't you? All those little nudges. The fires. The dreams. The moment they met... that was you."

"Of course it was me," I whisper, dipping my bloody hand into the heart of the sigil. The stone beneath pulses like flesh. The entire forest breathes with me. "I *wrote* their obsession before they ever touched. I carved it into the bones of the world."

Nibbles lets out a low whistle. "You're the horniest destiny goblin I've ever met."

"I'm not doing this for pleasure," I snap.

"You *should*. He's got that angry daddy energy."

"I'm doing this to maintain balance. Their union... their madness... it shifts the scale. Besides, I get myself off just fine without the weaving."

Without missing a beat Nibbles answers, "Oh I know, I've heard, even watched a few... hundred times. It's kinda hot... you get loud."

I just rolled my eyes at him. "I'm glad you enjoy the show" I snapped back.

He picks up a skull and mimics me in falsetto: "'Oh, I'm Elysandra, Guardian of the Realm, Spinner of Destiny, and I definitely don't fantasize about emotionally damaged warlords covered in blood and guilt.'"

I throw a candle at him.

He catches it in his mouth and eats it.

"Look," he says through a mouthful of wax, "I know you're all fate and secrets and shadowy bitch goddess of the forest, but maybe... and hear me out, you let yourself *enjoy* this once in a while. Go touch grass. Or touch Kael. Or Bethany. Or both."

I narrow my eyes.

He freezes.

"Ohhhhhhhhh," he drawls, toothy grin spreading. "Is that a *blush*, m'lady? You got it bad for the lady-in-waiting, don't you?"

"Silence," I growl.

"Oh, I *knew* it! All those longing looks and mysterious smirks. You wanna do unspeakable things to her with vines and enchanted oils!"

I hurl the ritual knife at him. It misses by a hair and sinks into the pillar with a satisfying *thunk*.

He doesn't flinch.

"Love you too," he chirps.

I roll my eyes and finish the weaving. The runes seal themselves shut with a sound like breaking ice. The power takes hold, deeper than blood, louder than thought.

Kael and Seraphina will not survive this untouched. But they will *burn*. And the world will shift with them.

"I don't need love," I murmur.

Nibbles waddles closer, tilting his head. "Sure. Keep telling yourself that, Fate-Mommy."

He farts.

The circle flares with light.

And for the first time in a century, I genuinely laugh.

CHAPTER XIX
ASHES OF THE HEART

SERAPHINA

The room was suffocating. Flickering candlelight painted trembling shadows across the cold, stone walls of my chamber. The embers in the hearth were dying, casting more darkness than warmth. My riding cloak lay crumpled on the chair like discarded guilt, its edges stained with traces of snowmelt from the night's reckless ride. The scent of sweat, leather, and faint traces of pine clung to me like a secret... *his* scent. I paced, back and forth, my bare feet brushing against the cool stones, trying to silence the roaring in my head. My heart hadn't stopped racing since I left him... since Kael's hands had been on my skin, his breath mingling with mine under that moonlit sky.

The memory of his voice echoed like a prayer I couldn't unhear: *"My heart beats for you now. It belongs to you."* I bit down on my lip until I tasted copper, desperate to ground myself. But nothing could drown him out. Bethany sat in silence, her face shadowed with exhaustion, her brows knit tight like she'd been waiting to ambush me. She didn't bother with the usual pleasantries. No soft smile. No gentle questions. Just her sitting there, arms crossed, her gaze as sharp as a blade.

"Where the *fuck* have you been?" she snapped, slamming the door shut behind her. I froze mid-step, my heart stumbling. She'd never spoken to me like that before. Not Bethany. Not my confidante. My friend. But here she was, her voice trembling, not from fear, but from fury. I turned slowly, lifting my chin, swallowing down the immediate urge to lie. But the words burned my throat. What was the point? She already knew.

"That's none of your concern," I replied coolly, masking the chaos boiling inside me. Her eyes narrowed; her jaw clenched.

"None of my concern?" She stood up, her boots echoing like distant drums. "*None of my concern?* You sneak out like a thief in the night, and I'm the one covering for you. I'm the one lying to guards, to the staff... to your *father*, so you can go... What? Risk your life for *him*?" I flinched at the word. *Him.* Spoken with such disdain, like Kael was nothing more than a passing thought, a foolish mistake.

"Don't you *dare* speak about him like that," I hissed, my voice low and trembling. "You don't know anything about him." Bethany laughed bitterly, a hollow, sharp sound that cut through me.

"Oh, I know enough. He's the man who's turned you into someone I barely recognize." I took a step forward, my chest heaving.

"You mean someone who finally feels *alive*?" Her mouth opened, but I didn't give her the chance. "I don't just love him, Bethany... I *belong* to him." My voice cracked, raw with the truth I'd been choking on. "My skin, my soul, every fucking breath I take... *They are his!*" Silence followed, thick and suffocating. Bethany's face softened for a brief moment before hardening again. She shook her head, her voice lowering to a trembling whisper.

"You're going to get yourself killed." I felt a laugh bubble up, hysterical and wild.

"*So, what if I do?*" Her eyes widened in disbelief.

"Do you even hear yourself? You're not thinking clearly!"

"Oh, I'm thinking *perfectly* clearly," I snapped, stepping closer until we were nose to nose. "I'd rather choke on the ashes of this kingdom than breathe another day without *him*." Bethany recoiled like I'd slapped her. Her eyes glistened, but she blinked the tears away, refusing to show weakness. Not now. Not with me unraveling in front of her.

"Seraphina, please." Her voice softened, filled with something I couldn't stand... *pity*. "This isn't love. This is... Obsession. It's poison." I clenched my fists so tightly my nails dug into my palms, leaving crescent-shaped marks.

"Then let it fucking kill me." She grabbed my arm, shaking me with a force that stunned me. "I'm trying to *save* you!" I yanked my arm free, my chest rising and falling with ragged breaths.

"I don't need saving." I went black, as if nothing else existed around me, Bethany's words lingered in my mind. Her disdain of *My* King. It was like an infection spreading through my thoughts... 'til I snapped. I grabbed Bethany by her shoulder and slammed her against the cold, stone wall. The same walls that felt as if they were closing in on me. I stared her in the eyes as I drew my dagger from the scabbard on my thigh and placed it to her throat. "I swear to the Gods, Bethany, with the very breath I breathe. If you speak of *My* King with such disrespect again, I *will* kill you." Bethany's face crumpled, her composure finally cracking.

"I don't want to lose you." Tears welled in my eyes, hot and blinding.

"Then figure out who's side you are on." The words hung there, venomous and true. She sank into the chair by the hearth, her hands trembling as she buried her face in them. I stood there, breathing like I'd just fought a battle... and in a way, I had. The war was inside me. After a long, heavy silence, Bethany lifted her head, her voice barely above a whisper. "Would you *really* die for him?" I didn't hesitate.

"I'd slit my own throat with a smile if he asked me to... For *him*, even death feels like *devotion*."

Bethany's face went pale, the color draining like I'd stabbed her with those words. She realized then, there was no saving me. I was already gone. She stood slowly, her eyes glossy but defiant.

"I hope he's worth it." I didn't answer. To me, he wasn't just *worth* it. *He was everything.* She left without another word, the door clicking shut like the final nail in a coffin. I sank to the floor, my back against the cold stone, the silence pressing down like a weight. I whispered his name into the dark.

Kael.

The sound of it didn't feel like enough.

CHAPTER XX
THE POINT OF NO RETURN

The heavy wooden door slammed shut behind Bethany, the sound reverberating through my chambers like the last breath of a dying thing. My fingers curled into the silken fabric of my gown, twisting it tight as I tried to steady the storm raging inside of me. My chest heaved, my pulse a wild drumbeat in my throat.

She doesn't fucking understand.

Bethany's words still hung in the air, suffocating me. The way she had looked at me; her expression shifting between concern and judgment, made my skin crawl. I pressed my forehead against the cold, stone wall, my breath coming in quick, shallow gasps. My body trembled, not just with frustration, but with something else. Something dark. Something that whispered; *go to him.*

161

Kael.

His name alone was enough to set me ablaze, to make my knees weak and my skin itch for his touch. The memory of him, of his hands gripping me, his voice rasping in my ear, had been tormenting me since the moment I left his camp.

"I need to see him. I need to fucking see him." My fingers twitched toward the laces of my gown. I had to change. I had to get out of here before... A voice slithered through the chamber, low and amused.

"Quite the little firestorm, aren't you?" My breath hitched, my entire body going rigid. I turned sharply, my pulse hammering in my throat. And there, standing at the edge of the dying firelight, was a woman draped in shadows. She was dangerous, beauty incarnate... tall and poised, her red hair cascading down her back like liquid fire, her emerald eyes gleaming with something knowing, something ancient.

"Who the fuck are you?" I snapped, the edge in my voice betraying the unease twisting inside of me. Her lips curled into a slow, wicked grin.

"Such a mouth on you, Princess. And here I thought Eldorian nobility were taught restraint." My fingers flexed at my sides, itching for the dagger I kept in the scabbard on my thigh...

"I don't have patience for games."

"Oh, but you do, little one." Her voice was velvet and steel, seductive and lethal. "You're playing the most dangerous one of all. And I must say... It's been delightful to watch." Her words sent a chill slithering down my spine.

"You've been watching me? You are the one I saw a glimpse of in the forest, you're Elysandra aren't you!?" Her smirk widened, the flickering firelight casting jagged shadows across her sharp cheekbones.

"You truly have no idea, do you?"

ELYSANDRA

Gods, she was magnificent. A princess on the edge of ruin, her mind unraveling thread by thread, her heart bleeding for a man who would carve her name into the very fabric of history. *Obsession is such a beautiful thing to witness.*

"I haven't only been watching you, Princess," I said smoothly, stepping further into the dimly lit chamber. "I've been watching him, too." Her lips parted slightly, but no sound came. *Ah, there it is.* The realization. The *barest flicker of jealousy* beneath the storm in her eyes. "Oh, my dear girl," I purred, "you really think your love story has been unfolding in secrecy?" She swallowed hard, her fingers trembling at her sides. "I've seen every desperate glance. Every stolen touch. Every forbidden kiss."

"I don't give a fuck what you've seen," she spat. I laughed, a rich, dark sound that made her bristle.

"Of course you do," I crooned, circling her like a vulture. "You want to know what I've seen, don't you?" I leaned in, voice dropping to a whisper. "You want to know if he dreams of you." She exhaled shakily. "If his hands ache for you the way yours ache for him. "Her breath hitched. "If his mind is just as poisoned as yours." I grinned, watching her unravel before my eyes. "Tell me, little princess... What would you do to keep him?"

SERAPHINA

"Anything," I whispered. I didn't even have to think about it. Not my title. Not my kingdom. Not my crown. None of it fucking mattered anymore.

"That's what I thought," Elysandra mused, tilting her head. She circled me like a predator toying with its prey, her emerald eyes watching my every move.

"What are you?" I finally asked. She grinned, slow and wicked. "I am Elysandra, the Witch of the Eldorian Forest. Guardian of the unseen. Weaver of fates. And, my dear, I have lived long enough to know when a story is worth watching unfold." My chest tightened.

"And ours is worth watching?" Her smile sharpened.

"Oh, my dear... I don't just watch. I shape."

ELYSANDRA

I reached out, trailing my fingers down her *delicate throat,* feeling the *pulse that thundered beneath my touch.*

"You are not meant to be caged in this kingdom, Seraphina." Her lashes fluttered. "You were born to be ruined by love, to be devoured by it, to let it consume you whole." I leaned in close, my voice a breath against her ear. "Go to him, Princess. Let him claim you piece by piece." She *let out a shuddered breath*, her pupils blown wide, her body trembling. "And when the world starts to burn around you, remember this moment." I grinned. "Because darling... I will be watching."

SERAPHINA

Elysandra pulled back, leaving me *cold, raw, exposed*. I wanted to *deny her words*. I wanted to *cling to logic*. I wanted to *pretend I could still be the woman I was supposed to be*. But I wasn't that woman anymore. I was *Kael's*. I was *his*.

"Get out," I breathed. Elysandra chuckled softly, stepping back into the shadows.

"Oh, my sweet girl," she purred, disappearing into the darkness. "You don't want me gone. You just don't want to hear the truth."

And then she was gone. I stood there for a long moment, the weight of my choice *suffocating* and *thrilling* all at once. Then, I turned. I grabbed my cloak. And I *ran into the night*. Straight to *Kael*.

CHAPTER XXI
TEMPTING FATE

P ower smells like sweat and desperation.

That's what hit me first when I stepped into Alaric's chambers without so much as a knock. A thick musk of overindulgence, spilled wine, and the kind of masculine pride that thinks a cock and a crown are interchangeable.

He didn't notice me right away. Of course he didn't.

He was lying in bed, sheets lazily draped over his hips, one leg exposed, a goblet in one hand and the smirk of a man who believes the world has already bent over for him.

The firelight flickered over his oiled chest... yes, oiled, as if the glistening sheen of self-worship might make him more kingly, and his cockiness was on full display beneath the fabric. Not that he was fully hard... yet. That would take more effort than I had patience for. Fortunately, tonight, I was willing to invest.

He turned his head, finally noticing me as I emerged from the shadows.

"What the...? Gods, woman. You trying to kill me?" He sat up, the blanket falling lower. "How long have you been standing there?"

"Long enough," I said flatly, walking into the light with slow, deliberate steps.

He didn't blink. Didn't speak. Just gave me that look... lazy, lecherous, the kind of grin that oozed from every man who thought power was a game of bedsheets and bloodlines.

"You've got a talent for drama," he said, setting the goblet aside and reclining again, arms folded behind his head like a painting of misplaced confidence. "Don't tell me you've finally come to your senses. Realized you'd rather be my mistress than my menace."

I raised an eyebrow. "You think I came here to fuck you?"

He laughed... an arrogant bark that made my teeth ache.

"Come now. You've haunted these halls for decades, like some brooding ghost. You can't tell me you've never thought about it. About climbing into bed with power."

I walked to the hearth, letting the flames warm my palms. I didn't look at him yet. He hadn't earned it.

"Alaric," I said calmly, "you mistake my silence for interest. That's adorable."

He shifted beneath the covers, his cock likely twitching to the idea of conquest, not realizing he was the one being hunted.

"Adorable, huh?" he said. "Well, maybe you should crawl into bed and find out just how adorable I can be."

I turned slowly. Gave him a long look. The kind that dissects, not flirts.

"You're ambitious," I said. "You want the throne. You want your name carved into the stones of history."

"Is this where you tell me I'm unworthy?" he smirked.

"Oh no," I purred, stepping closer. "This is where I tell you... I might be inclined to help."

That made him sit up straighter. The sheet shifted again, gods help us, the man had no shame.

"Help?" he repeated, voice dipped in sudden caution.

"You want it all," I said, circling the bed like a vulture. "The title. The glory. The songs. You want to be the man who rebuilt Eldoria from the ashes."

He nodded slowly, the first glimmer of sincerity flickering in his eyes.

"And I want," I continued, "to see whether you can carry that burden without drowning in your own ego."

"Try me."

I paused at the foot of his bed.

He licked his lips.

I let the silence stretch.

And then, finally, I reached behind me. Fingers found the laces of my corset. I didn't rush it. I wanted him to watch. I wanted him to think he'd won something.

The garment slid off me like the peeling of a second skin, pooling around my ankles.

His eyes widened, but not with respect. With hunger.

I crawled onto the bed, deliberately slow, moving like smoke and sin. He shifted to meet me, that smug expression turning downright feral.

He had no idea the web already had him.

I crawled slowly. I watched his eyes scan my body like he was a starving man in the desert. I watched his eyes lock onto my ass as I was slowly moving forward. As I reached the blanket covering his cock... I had noticed that he had started to get hard. I smiled at him. This arrogant man... had gotten hard before I even touched him. This was going to be far easier than I thought.

I slipped what was left of the velvet sheet covering his cock off to the side. As I pulled the sheet to the side, his manhood bounced out from under it lightly tapping me on the chin. As I suspected, his cock didn't match his ego. It was serviceable enough though. Not a complete disappointment.

I intentionally locked eyes with him as I slowly wrapped my fingers around his cock. I smiled as I started to slowly stroke up... and down. My grip getting slightly tighter each time. He started thrusting his hips as I stroked.

I let out an evil, girlish giggle as he let out a light moan. I noticed his pre-cum starting to pool up on the head of his cock. I stuck my tongue out and slowly swirled it around the head. As I retracted my tongue, one strand of his precum bridged from the head to my tongue. As I closed my lips around my tongue, the strand broke, hitting my chin.

"That tastes... sweet". I moaned at him. As I licked my lips his precum gave me an idea for a ritual. I leaned over and gave the head of his cock a nice kiss and I smiled.

"That's all for now big boy". I grinned.

"That's it? You aren't even going to finish the job?" he scoffed.

He lay there afterward, sweat-slicked and stupid, trying to look smug through the fog of spent lust. His chest heaved.

I leaned down, brushing a finger against his jaw.

"If you want me to finish the job, I want you to meet me," I whispered, voice soft and cold, "at the edge of the Eldorian Forest. Dawn."

"Mmm?" he murmured. "To what... get another tease?"

I smiled, sharp, deadly. "To claim your future. I'll begin the ritual there. The one that will make your name eternal."

His brow furrowed. "Wait. Ritual?"

"You wanted to be remembered, Alaric. And I always keep my promises."

I stood, retrieving my corset with a lazy flick of my wrist. The shadows curled eagerly around my naked form like loyal hounds.

"You'll be there?" I asked, turning my head slightly over my shoulder.

He nodded. Still breathless. Still dumb.

"I'll be there."

"Good," I said, fastening the first lace. "I'd hate to have to come back."

Then I was gone, vanishing into the dark like the threat I was.

But the forest would remember.

And soon, so would he.

For as long as he lived.

Which, as fate would have it, may not be too long.

CHAPTER XXII
THE BINDING

ELYSANDRA

The Eldorian Forest is still at dawn. That kind of stillness that doesn't offer peace, just an uneasy hush, like the trees are holding their breath.

He came. Of course he did.

Alaric stepped out of the fog like a knight from a child's bedtime tale, all polished pride and puffed-up ambition. Cloak drawn, chin high, cocky smirk locked in place like he thought it made him look dangerous instead of foolish. He's late, and I suspect it's on purpose. Some pathetic attempt to seem mysterious. As if I hadn't already seen the whole pathetic arc of his life before he even crawled out of the womb.

"Elysandra," he said, like he was greeting a lover. "You're even more radiant by morning light."

I rolled my eyes so hard I'm surprised they didn't pop out of my skull. "And you still reek of desperation, Alaric. Shall we begin?"

He tried to laugh it off, brushing hair from his eyes like he thought it would charm me. I didn't bother pretending to flirt. That would've been a mercy.

Instead, I turned and extended a hand. "Come. You want to be remembered, don't you?"

He hesitated, just for a second. His ego wanted to ask questions, but the part of him that believed he was born to rule tugged his limbs forward. He took my hand.

I led him through twisted paths no sane soul walks willingly. The forest opened for me like a wound, ancient and pulsing with secrets it should've long since been buried. My sanctuary was waiting.

It's not a place you find on any map. Vines twisted into walls. Bones laced through bark. The scent of iron and incense danced together, biting and sweet. Torches flared to life as we stepped in, casting flickering shadows on runes carved into every surface. This was no ordinary ritual space—it was an altar of endings.

Alaric looked around, visibly impressed and barely trying to hide the arousal blooming under his belt. "This is... ancient," he muttered, reverent for once. "Powerful."

"Powerful enough to rewrite fate," I whispered.

He stood in the center, just as I willed, eyes drinking in every dark corner while I moved around him. I lit the final candle and unsheathed my obsidian dagger from the folds of my cloak. The metal drank the light greedily. I didn't flinch as I dragged it across my skin, once on my forearm, once over my sternum, and one final time along my thigh.

Blood trickled down in elegant rivers, hot and red, like liquid threads of destiny unraveling around me.

Alaric stepped closer. "This is what power looks like," he said, almost in awe.

"No," I said, catching his gaze as I smirked. "This is what *control* looks like."

I stepped into the center of the circle, drawing sigils on the floor with my own blood. The forest responded, groaning, the wind shifting in unnatural pulses. I could feel the world bending slightly, just slightly, under the weight of what I was weaving.

I turned to him and let the corset fall, slowly this time. Not as an offering, but a trap dressed as desire.

He bit down a groan. "This is the legacy I was promised..."

"Indeed," I whispered. "Undress and lay in the center of the circle." I commanded.

I watched as Alaric eagerly disrobed himself, 'til he was standing in the center of the circle with the smirk of an ass and the hard cock of a horny teenage boy.

"Lay here? In the dirt?" he questioned.

"Yes, lay down there in the center" I smirked.

I watched again as he fumbled around and finally laid down in the center of the circle. I toyed with the idea of fucking with him further, but honestly, I didn't want him here no longer than he needed to be.

I waved my hand, and roots came out of the ground. They wrapped around his wrists... and then his ankles. Now, he was immobile. Right where I wanted him.

"Naughty girl I see, I like it. Make good with your promise, Witch. I don't know how much more teasing I can handle". He commanded.

I smirked as I positioned myself over top of him. I stood there as he drank in my beauty.

"Patience is not one of your virtues, is it?" I asked rhetorically.

I stood there for a few moments longer. I glanced down at Alaric's cock; it was hard and already throbbing. I knew this wouldn't take too long. As I was standing there over top of him, I noticed blood had started to drip onto him from my cuts. I smiled at him as I crouched down.

I reached under me, and I grabbed his cock. I slapped it against my pussy a few times. He let out a slight groan of pleasure as I did. I just smirked at him. I pressed his cock against my pussy and I lifted my hips. His cock slid down my pussy and I kept going with it, until it reach my ass. I took a deep breath and pressed his cock into my ass slowly.

"Ooohhhhh, we are doing it that way...." He moaned.

As the head of his cock slowly slid into my ass, I finally dropped down to my knees. I leaned over and looked him in the eyes.

"I wouldn't give you my pussy if you were one of the Gods..." I laughed. "I hope you didn't think you were THAT lucky, I said I'd fuck you... I didn't say how."

I laughed for a few moments as I sat down further on his cock. That statement never rang more true than it does right now. He was getting fucked alright... in more ways than he could fathom.

As I sat all the way down on Alaric's cock, he let out a loud moan.

"Aaahhhhh yes, Witch. That's it... go all the way down on it."

As if he thought he had a massive cock or something... I laughed a little more inside. I'll have to admit, not having any cock at all in over 70 years... did feel kind of nice... So, I indulged in his ego fueled fantasy. I pressed my hips down onto his cock as hard as I could press, pushing his cock as deep into my ass as it would go.

I leaned back and put my hands onto his thighs to give him a great show of what he wasn't getting. By this time... my blood was smeared all over his chest and his stomach. It was glorious. I enjoyed the sight so much, I even let out a few loud moans as he thrust his hips and cock in and out of my ass.

Our bodies shimmered in the crimson of my blood in the candlelight. It was arousing. I kept moving my hips back and forth... faster and faster... I kept looking at our bodies... smeared in blood. I started moaning... not necessarily from Alaric's cock in my ass, but from a combination of the two.

I grabbed my blood-soaked breast and pinched my nipple between my fingers 'til I felt pain...

"Ooohhh, Gods!" I let out uncontrollably. I was actually having an orgasm... "AHHHHHHHH!!! FFUUUCCKKKK!" I screamed.

My body started to convulse... shaking uncontrollably... I rocked my hips harder... and harder... I felt my ass muscles tightening around Alaric's cock with each convulsion. I kept going...

"Ahhh yes, Witch. Give that ass to me!" Alaric moaned.

My body kept shaking... my legs had no more strength in them... so I dropped back down to my knees. I kept going... I kept rocking my hips... harder and harder. I was cumming again!

"OOOHHHHHH FUUCCKKK!" I screamed again. As I orgasmed... I felt my nails dig into Alaric's chest. My body was shaking so hard... I couldn't hardly breathe. I looked up at Alaric's chest and I had drawn his blood with my clawing.

Alaric started thrusting his hips... harder and harder... I could feel his cock beginning to swell in my ass. He was getting ready to cum. He kept thrusting...

"OOOHHH GODS, I'm going to cum, Witch!" he moaned out loud.

I lifted my hips up and felt his cock slide out of my ass... I grabbed his cock in my hand and stroked it hard and fast.

"AAHHHHHH!" He screamed.

With each stroke, ropes of his cum shot from his cock onto his chest and stomach. I kept stroking him. His body shook, his hips kept thrusting.

Finally, he had calmed down and I turned the death grip I had on his cock loose. I reach for a bowl I had prepared for the ritual, and I scooped up his cum and my blood from his chest and his stomach. I stood up... my legs and knees still shaking. I walked around the ritual circle. I dipped my finger into the bowl, and I traced my cum and blood-soaked finger over each rune around the circle. As I did each rune, they lit up in a green hue. As I traced the last, the roots and vines that had Alaric bound, retracted into the ground freeing him.

Still trying to catch my breath I said, "And with that, the ritual is complete... and we have a deal, Alaric."

"For a witch, you sure do know how to ride a cock." He pridefully said.

"Don't toot your own horn big boy, I had to get myself off. I don't have another 900 years to wait on you." I snapped.

His breathing was ragged, body slick with sweat, skin marked by my sigils, his essence now part of the blood-slicked ritual spiraling across the forest floor.

I stood and looked down at him, my hands stained with crimson, my skin gleaming with sweat and magic. Alaric lay back in the dirt like he thought he had just fucked his way into the history books.

And in a way, he had.

He would be remembered. Just not the way he believed.

"You did well," I murmured, brushing his cheek with a tenderness I did not feel. "Your name will echo through Eldoria."

"Will?" he asked, lips curling. "You mean it already doesn't?"

Oh, darling. *That's the point.*

I smiled and leaned down, kissed his forehead gently. "Go, now. Rest. Tomorrow begins your rise."

He left with a strut in his step and the stink of triumph clinging to his skin like cheap perfume.

I stayed behind, alone in the circle, letting the blood dry on my skin. My fingers brushed the runes I'd carved into the floor, his name already unraveling in them, twisted and mangled, never to be spoken by history's lips.

"You'll be forgotten," I whispered into the smoke. "By my hand, by her flame. And the world will never know why."

CHAPTER XXIII
THE TIES THAT BIND

ELYSANDRA

The blood had dried sticky across my hips, a dark maroon smear over flesh that no longer bled. I stood in the center of the circle, the symbols still glowing faintly beneath my bare feet... sigils carved into the ancient stone with my own damn lifeblood. The ritual had taken hold the moment he came, the moment I drew the sigils on the stone and his seed mixed with my blood.

He thought he'd conquered me.

He thought the gods themselves had parted the heavens to crown his cock.

I exhaled slowly. The air in the sanctuary tasted of iron, incense, sweat, and smoke. The torches along the wall flickered, casting long shadows that curled like fingers across the runes.

"Damn, Mistress."

I didn't turn. I didn't need to. The voice came from above, cheeky, rough, gleeful.

"You let that fool rail you like he was one of the Gods reborn."

The clatter of claws on stone, and then the warm, foul breath of my favorite parasite ghosted over my shoulder.

"Nibbles," I said without emotion, raising a blood-soaked hand to wipe my neck. "You always come crawling out when the scent is fresh."

"Hard not to when the air's full of butt sex and sorcery." He landed beside me with a crunch of bone and dirt. "And you... standing there with his cum on your hands, looking like a goddess sculpted from war crimes."

I rolled my eyes. "You watched the whole thing, didn't you?"

"Watched?" he snorted. "I damn near needed a second dick. That was *hot*. And you came twice... don't lie to me, Mistress. I *counted*."

I bent to pick up the cloth I'd set aside earlier. The motion pulled a line of drying blood down my thigh. "Of course I did. Why shouldn't I get some enjoyment out of it?"

Nibbles chuckled like a demon choking on lust. "That's my girl. Fucked him *and* fucked him over. You should give lessons."

"Too much effort," I muttered, wiping the blood off my stomach. "And the students would never survive."

He hopped up onto a broken pillar, perching like a gargoyle with a smirk. "I mean, credit where it's due, Alaric really thought he was sealing his legacy with that load. Gods, the look on his face when you told him to lay down. Fucking priceless."

I tossed the cloth into the fire. It hissed like a dying thing. "Let him believe it. Let him march back into that keep with a hard-on and the scent of me on his body. He thinks he fucked his way to a crown."

"Meanwhile," Nibbles drawled, "you just stamped his name off the scroll of history and wrote 'coward' over it in blood."

I walked toward the basin. Water shimmered as I waved my hand over it, cleansing magic blooming in slow spirals. My skin healed beneath my fingertips. The ritual wounds sealed. No scars. No evidence. Not that I ever needed an alibi.

"I'm impressed you didn't kill him," Nibbles said behind me. "You've slit throats for less than a stupid smirk."

"He's more useful alive... for now," I said. "Every step has to be perfectly timed. One misstep and Seraphina's path cracks. This was necessary."

I turned, robes stitching themselves together from threads of shadow and silk, winding around my body like obedient vipers.

"But I *am* curious," I said, narrowing my eyes at him. "How many times did you jerk off while watching?"

"Just once," Nibbles said, raising his claw. "But it lasted the whole damn ritual. Very efficient. Almost spiritual... brought a tear to my eye."

I snorted, tightening the clasp at my collar. "At least you'll have material for later."

"Too late for that shit," he grinned. "I finished halfway through and kept going just for fun."

"You're vile."

"I'm *honest*. Big difference."

I walked back to the center of the ritual circle. The runes underfoot pulsed once, subtle, deliberate, obedient.

The magic held.

The binding was sealed.

Alaric's fate was no longer his own.

He'd spilled his seed into a ritual that would never bear him legacy, into a throne that would never hold his name, into a legend that would swallow him whole and spit out ash.

"History won't remember him," I whispered.

Nibbles tilted his head. "But you will?"

"I remember everyone," I said. "Especially the ones who thought they mattered."

A silence stretched between us, thick and humming with power.

And then Nibbles grinned again. "Still. That was some *grade-A* ass fucking."

I stared at him, deadpan. "You want me to draw you a summoning circle so you can find a real partner?"

"Oh no," he cackled. "I like the free show. And your taste in men? *Chef's kiss.*"

I rolled my eyes and walked away.

Behind me, the ritual sigils faded into black stone, leaving nothing but silence, and the faint, lingering scent of ruin.

Everything was exactly as I planned.

And the end had already begun.

CHAPTER XXIV
WHISPERS IN THE DARK

BETHANY

T he moon was high, silver and cold, casting jagged beams of light through the frost-laced window of my chambers. My fingers clenched the hem of my sheets, knuckles white, my mind a tangled web of uncertainty and guilt. The fire in the hearth had burned low, offering only the faintest glow of embers against the darkness. I had barely moved since returning from Seraphina's chambers. The fight... Gods, the fight. The look in her eyes when she spoke of Kael... *possessed, devoted, damned.*

"I don't just love him, Bethany... I belong to him." Her words clung to me like a sickness, crawling beneath my skin. *"I'd rather choke on the ashes of this kingdom than breathe another day without him."* I squeezed my eyes shut, bile rising in my throat. I had never seen her like this before, had never seen her so *lost*, so *consumed*, and no matter how hard I tried to push her back from the edge, she just... Jumped headfirst into the abyss. And I was helpless to stop her.

"What am I supposed to do?" I whispered into the empty room.

"You could start by telling the truth." My heart slammed into my ribs as I whipped around, reaching for the dagger under my pillow... only to stop cold. A woman stood in the far corner of the room, half-bathed in shadow, watching me with a smile like a blade. Her hair was red as freshly spilled blood, cascading over the black folds of her gown, catching the moonlight like embers in the dark. Her emerald eyes gleamed, sharp as polished glass, filled with something unreadable, something ancient. A chill that had nothing to do with the cold crept up my spine.

"Who..." I swallowed, my voice a ghost in my throat. "You... You're her!" She took a single step forward, the candlelight flickering wildly as if afraid of her presence.

"Yes, Indeed I am... I am Elysandra," she purred, voice smooth as silk, sharp as steel. "The Witch of the Eldorian Forest. The weaver of fates. The whisper in the dark." She smiled, and the room felt smaller. "And I have come to speak with you, Bethany."

ELYSANDRA

Fear.

It radiated from her, thick and intoxicating, curling around the air like the smoke from dying embers. She tried to hide it behind anger, behind that fierce little glare, the way her fingers tightened around the sheets. But I saw through it. I saw everything.

Bethany, the loyal friend, the moral tether Seraphina had left behind in the wake of her obsession. A woman torn between duty and devotion.

How poetic.

"You're afraid," I mused, stepping closer, watching how her pulse jumped in her throat. "You think she's lost to you. You think she's drowning." Her jaw clenched. "You don't know whether to throw her a rope... Or let her fucking sink." Bethany flinched, eyes burning as she shot up from the bed.

"You don't know a fucking thing about me." I smiled.

"Oh, little dove, I know everything about you."

BETHANY

The way she said it made my blood run cold. I stepped back, pulse hammering, my mind screaming for me to run, but my feet wouldn't fucking move.

"I don't know what the hell you want, but..." I swallowed.

"You can tell Seraphina whatever the fuck you're planning, I'm not going to..."

"Seraphina doesn't need to know." My mouth snapped shut." This conversation is between us, Bethany. No one else." The way she said my name made my stomach churn. "I've been watching you." She circled me like a predator, her voice dripping with amusement. "Listening. Waiting."

"For what?" I whispered. Her smile was wicked, predatory.

"For you to break."

ELYSANDRA

Bethany was cracking, but she wasn't shattered yet. She still clung to the idea that she had control, that her loyalty would be enough to save Seraphina. But I had seen too many like her before. People who thought they could stop what was already set in motion.

"You're struggling, Bethany," I murmured, tilting my head. "Torn between protecting her and betraying her." Her hands curled into fists.

"I'd never fucking betray her." I smiled.

"No?" I stepped closer, lowering my voice to a whisper. "Then why does it feel like you already have?" She froze. A shuddering breath escaped her lips, her eyes darting away. Good.

BETHANY

I felt like I was suffocating. She was inside my head, picking apart the pieces I had tried to hold together. And I fucking hated her for it. "You have two choices," Elysandra said, voice like velvet wrapping around my throat.

"You can tell the King what you know and sleep soundly knowing you did what was expected of you." My stomach twisted. "Or..." She lifted my chin gently, but there was nothing soft in her touch. "You can take fate into your own hands." I stared at her, breath coming fast.

"And how the fuck do I do that?" Her smile darkened.

"Let me show you."

ELYSANDRA

The deal was made. She didn't know it yet.

But she would. Soon.

"Choose wisely, little dove." I leaned in, whispering against her ear, my voice curling like smoke around her mind. "Because one path leads to fire..." I pulled back, grinning. "And the other?" I ran a single nail down her jaw, feeling her shudder beneath my touch. "To ashes." And then, I was gone.

Vanishing into the shadows. Leaving behind only the echo of my words... And the sound of Bethany's ragged breath.

CHAPTER XXV
THE WEAVER'S CURSE

ELYSANDRA

I knew pain.

Not the fleeting kind. Not the kind that healed. But the kind that stayed. The kind that whispered in the night. The kind that dug its claws into the marrow of my bones and never let go. The kind that turned little girls into something else.

My mother's screams still haunted my dreams. The smell of burning flesh, the wails of a woman being devoured by flames... *all for the crime of loving her child.* I had watched, a small thing barely five years old, clutching a doll with half its stuffing gone, as the people cheered.

"Witch-born! Demon-blood!" They had shouted. My mother had not begged for her life. She had only begged the gods to take me away from this cursed fate. But the gods did not listen. And when the fire reached her throat and cut her screams into silence, I felt the first crack inside my soul. I had been dragged to the altar like an animal, not to be killed, but to be bound. Bound to the Moonspire Circle. Bound to the curse that would never let me rest. A coven of witches, ancient as the forest itself. They had painted my naked body with symbols of the old gods. They had pressed a dagger to my wrist. They had opened my veins and poured me into fate's hands.

The Norns.

Past, Present, and Future. The unholy trinity of cunts I was to be bound to. But we all got much darker than we bargained for.

I had screamed until my voice was gone. But it hadn't been from pain.

No. It had been from the visions that ripped through my mind like shattered glass. I had seen it all. Every path, every future, every thread of fate stretching across eternity. And not a single one led to peace.

I saw myself burn. Over and over again. I saw myself beg for mercy that would never come. I saw myself falling, deeper, deeper, until there was nothing left of the girl I had once been. When it was over, I did not cry. Because there was no one left to cry for. I had emerged... something else. Immortal. Cursed to do the bidding of the Norns. But that wasn't all. Their ritual had unintended consequences. I was soul bound to Naglfar itself.

The ship made from skin, blood, and bone of the dead that ferried souls into the underworld. I had an added task... Lucky me.

I now was charged... with ferrying souls from this realm to the next and bound to the Eldorian Forest. Souls pass through my forest... they keep it lush. They keep it fed. And as long as the forest lives, I live. Someone has to do it. May as well be me.

My father had stood before me, triumphant. He had sold me to warlords and murderers, to men with hands stained red and hearts blackened with greed. I was to be their prize. A queen, they had called me. A whore, they had meant. And when I had refused to bow, refused to kneel, refused to be their pawn, I had destroyed them all. I burned their houses. I burned their temples. I burned their children. I had bathed the Moonspire witches in fire. I had carved out the heart of the high priestess and fed it to the crows. I had burned my father alive in his own throne. I had walked away from the ashes, barefoot and bloody, and never looked back. Afterall, *My* forest needed souls. It got plenty that day.

I stood in the darkness now; A cursed Moonspire witch, watching history repeat itself. Watching Seraphina. The princess was a fool. Or was she? A foolish, desperate girl who thought she had a choice. Who thought love was something soft, something beautiful. Who thought obsession was devotion. She was wrong. Or was she? I knew, but did she?

197

Love was a cage. And Seraphina had already stepped inside, locked the door, and thrown away the key. I had let her. I had whispered the right words, pressed the right wounds, deepened the right scars. Because Seraphina was meant for this. For ruin. For destruction. For greatness.

I followed her through the trees, my steps soundless over the snow. I watched as Seraphina entered Kael's tent. I watched as the firelight painted her skin in shades of gold and sin. I watched as Kael pulled her close, their voices low, their hands desperate. Seraphina, beneath him, tangled in sweat and silk, her fingers clawing at Kael's back as if she was trying to consume him. As if she wants to devour him whole. And perhaps she does. I did not need to hear them. I already knew what they would say. I had seen this moment long before it ever happened.

I will give them credit; they do put on a good show. Even better than I had envisioned it.

Seraphina had not just fallen. She was consumed. And Kael would drown with her. I leaned against the tent, the shadows wrapping around me like an old lover, listening. Not to their words. But to the soft sighs, the moans, the broken gasps, the fevered whispers of a girl who had surrendered to her own undoing.

I smiled.

This was the moment I had been waiting for. The moment where fate became sealed. The moment where Seraphina ceased to be a princess and became something else entirely. Something dark. Something beautiful. Something I had woven with my own hands. I turned away, stepping back into the night, my laughter silent, my heart black with satisfaction. The story was set now.

And it is written in blood. As all great stories are.

CHAPTER XXVI
OATH OF OBEDIENCE

SERAPHINA

The moment I touched the scepter; I stopped thinking like a queen.

It wasn't just a relic. It was history... mine. My father's. My ancestors'. All their hands had touched this. All their lips had brushed its crown during their coronations, whispering promises to protect the realm.

And now I was stealing it.

I wrapped it in silk, tucked it beneath my cloak, and left the castle without a word. No guards. No escort. Just me and the weight of legacy strapped to the side of my saddle.

The wind bit into my face as I rode. The moon was high and hard above the trees, silvering the world in cold fire. My hands trembled, not from fear... but from anticipation.

Kael had sent no summons. He hadn't asked for the scepter. I'd brought it on my own. And I knew what that meant.

I didn't want to prove anything to my kingdom. I wanted to prove it to *him*.

He waited for me on the edge of the ruins. Always calm. Always still. The kind of stillness that came from absolute control, not of others, but of himself. His sword was sheathed. His arms folded across his chest. But his eyes burned the second they saw me.

I dismounted, heart pounding. "I brought it."

He said nothing at first. Just watched me unwrap it.

The obsidian gleamed beneath the moonlight, gold filigree swirling like roots around the shaft. The crest was smooth, worn from centuries of hands, of lips, of vows. My hands barely felt steady enough to hold it.

Kael stepped forward, slowly, until we were only a breath apart.

"You stole the soul of your kingdom," he said softly.

I nodded. "I brought it to you."

He took the scepter, turning it in his hand with a warrior's reverence. "I believe you," he murmured. "You've never lied to me. Not once. Take your crown off princess, you aren't here for me to worship, I am here to ruin you."

His gaze returned to mine. "You're mine, aren't you?"

"Yes," I whispered.

Not because I had to. Because I wanted it. Because it was true.

He reached up, gently brushing a strand of hair from my cheek. His touch was light, tender, completely at odds with the fire that lived behind his eyes.

"Then give yourself to me."

My breath hitched.

"Not with words. With action." He held out the scepter again. "With this."

I looked at it. I knew what he meant. He didn't have to say it.

And I didn't hesitate.

I didn't flinch.

I stepped back, slowly, hands trembling as I unfastened my cloak. It fell to the ground in a whisper. Beneath it, I wore only the silken underdress I'd slept in... thin, sheer, clinging to the shape of me with every movement.

Kael didn't move. Didn't speak.

He simply watched.

And I... I loved it.

I knelt.

Not because he ordered me to. Because I *wanted* him to see me this way. Vulnerable. Willing. Devoted.

I took the scepter into my hands, cradling it like something sacred.

The moonlight caught the edges of it as I leaned back on my knees, spreading them slowly, reverently. The cool air kissed my skin. My pulse pounded in my ears. But I didn't falter.

Kael didn't blink.

He just whispered, "Show me."

I brought the crown of the scepter between my thighs.

It was cold... at first.

But I was already warm. Already slick. Already aching from nothing more than his eyes on me.

I moved slowly, guiding the relic of my bloodline into the place that now belonged only to him. My head fell back. My lips parted. And I moaned... not in shame, but in pleasure.

I loved this.

I loved him watching me.

I loved that he'd asked me to do this, and I loved that I had obeyed.

The scepter was smooth, hard, heavy in my grip. It slid deeper, and I gasped, arching into it. Every inch of pressure made me feel more exposed, more claimed, more *his*.

Kael stepped forward.

Still silent.

Still calm.

His eyes darkened with heat, but he didn't touch me.

That was the torment.

That was the gift.

He let me unravel for him... *only* for him.

I rocked my hips against the relic, every motion wet, desperate, beautiful. My moans filled the space between us, wild and un-restrained. I didn't care about the trees. About the stars. About anything but the man standing over me with eyes that said: *You are everything I want.*

I met his gaze and held it.

"I want you to see me," I said, voice trembling. "Like this. I want you to know... this body, this soul, this pleasure, *it belongs to you.*"

His voice came like thunder: "It always has."

The crest pressed deeper inside me. My thighs trembled. I gasped, head falling forward, body writhing against the stone beneath me.

Kael knelt.

And still didn't touch me.

But he whispered: "Don't stop."

I didn't.

I gave myself to the moment. To him. To the fire between my legs and the weight of the scepter inside me, the artifact of kings now defiled by a queen who no longer gave a damn about crowns.

I cried out, body arching, pleasure tearing through me like lightning. My back bowed, sweat slicking my skin. The scepter slipped from my hand as I collapsed forward... boneless, trembling, euphoric.

Kael caught it before it hit the ground.

He looked down at me.

"You've just rewritten history," he said softly.

I smiled, still panting. "Then let the bards write it well."

He leaned in. His lips brushed mine. Soft. Possessive. Full of the fire that hadn't cooled in him one bit.

"You're mine, Seraphina," he said. "Not because I took you. Because you gave yourself freely."

"I did," I whispered.

And I would again.

A hundred times over.

CHAPTER XXVII
LOYALTY BLEEDS FIRST

BETHANY

S he didn't come back until dawn.

Boots muddy. Eyes glazed over with that kind of post-sin glow people write bad poetry about.

She said nothing.

Didn't look at me.

Didn't even bother with the lie.

That was the worst part.

Seraphina had always told me *everything*. Now? I couldn't tell if I was her handmaiden, her protector, or just a piece of furniture she no longer noticed.

And I knew exactly who she'd gone to.

Kael. The enemy. The warmonger. The man who had already taken half the realm's blood... and now he had her body, too.

And I stood there. Silent. Obedient. Still.

Like a fucking fool.

ELYSANDRA

Gods, I love the smell of emotional breakdowns in the morning.

Bethany stalked the halls like someone wound too tight for her own good. Hair braided too neat. Boots too loud. She was radiating fury, guilt, and barely contained violence.

It was perfect.

I slipped from the shadows; because of course I did... and fell into step beside her like I'd always been there.

"Rough night?" I purred.

She didn't look at me.

Didn't need to.

I could see it on her face. She was a woman teetering on the edge of turning *loyalty into treason.*

Excellent.

BETHANY

I didn't even flinch when she appeared. I was too used to it.

Elysandra was like a bad habit you couldn't shake. The kind you hated yourself for indulging. She slinked through shadows like they owed her... and always seemed to show up right when you were trying not to fall apart.

"Don't start," I snapped.

"Start what?" she asked, all wide eyes and poison. "I haven't said a thing."

"You're thinking it."

She smirked. "Thinking *many* things. None of them helpful. All of them fun."

I stopped walking.

Turned to face her.

"You knew she went to him."

Her smile didn't falter. "I know *everything*."

ELYSANDRA

I tilted my head. Bethany was bristling like a wolf caught in its own trap.

Good.

"I'm guessing she didn't send a postcard," I said. "Just vanished into the woods, came back smelling like someone else's crown?"

She flinched.

Not because of the words, but because they were true.

"You think this is a game," she muttered.

"Oh no," I said, stepping in close, voice velvet. "This is the endgame."

Bethany clenched her jaw. "She's not herself."

I leaned in closer. "Or maybe this is who she's *always* been, and you're just now seeing it."

BETHANY

No. That wasn't true.

Seraphina wasn't reckless. She wasn't cruel.

She was brilliant. Stubborn. Loyal to a fault.

But this?

This obsession with Kael?

This *blindness*?

It was eating her alive; and if she kept going, it would eat the rest of us too.

"She's going to destroy herself," I said. "And she's going to take this kingdom down with her."

Elysandra's grin softened, just a little. "Now you're paying attention."

211

ELYSANDRA

I've waited *weeks* for her to wake up.

Bethany wasn't a fool. She was a warrior in servant's clothing. Fierce. Steady. Loyal like iron.

But loyalty was a knife. And knives could cut more than just enemies.

"She trusts him more than you," I said, gentle now.

Bethany looked away. "I know."

"And still, you say nothing."

"I'm not a traitor."

"No," I said. "You're a coward."

That got her. I saw it... like a slap across the soul.

BETHANY

"I've protected her through assassins, rebellions, political sabotage-"

Elysandra raised a brow. "But not from herself."

I wanted to hit her.

Wanted to scream.

But the truth was screaming louder inside me.

I'd watched Seraphina crumble under the weight of the crown for years. I'd seen her pulled between duty and emotion, seen her bleed behind closed doors just to keep the façade alive.

But now?

She wasn't crumbling.

She was changing.

And I didn't know what the hell was going to be left of her when Kael was done.

ELYSANDRA

"You could stop it," I said.

Bethany stared at me.

"You have the truth. You have the king's ear. You know where she goes. Who she sees."

Her hands were fists now.

"She'd never forgive me."

"She'd be alive," I said simply. "The kingdom might be intact. And Kael? He'd be dead."

Bethany's silence was almost enough to make me moan.

She was close.

So close to falling.

214

BETHANY

It felt like choosing between drowning and setting the boat on fire.

"I don't want her dead," I said.

Elysandra shrugged. "You want her safe. Pick your poison."

I stared at the hallway ahead.

The throne room wasn't far.

One report. One whisper. And this whole thing would collapse.

Kael would die.

Seraphina would fall.

And maybe... just maybe... Eldoria would survive.

ELYSANDRA

215

I stepped back into the shadows, voice low and wicked.

"You don't need to make a decision today."

Bethany didn't turn around.

"But you will. Soon."

Then I was gone.

And she was alone.

BETHANY

The hallway stretched before me like a blade.

At the end: power. Loyalty. Treason.

I stood there, frozen, as the first real question in years clawed its way into my chest:

What if saving her meant betraying her?

And what if doing nothing... meant *losing everything*?

CHAPTER XXVIII
HEAVY IS THE HEART

BETHANY

I couldn't fucking breathe.

The corridor felt like it was closing in, every goddamn stone pressing on my chest. My boots echoed against the marble floor; each click like a hammer on my conscience. Every step screamed, *Traitor. Liar. Coward.*

I had never betrayed Seraphina. Not once. Not when the nobles whispered that she wasn't fit to rule. Not when Alaric smiled that snake-oil smile and tried to wrap her in silk chains. Not even when Kael started showing up in her eyes like a damn fever dream... pulling her further away from us, from me, with every stolen glance and midnight escape.

But today? I was going to sell her out.

I stopped outside the King's chamber. The two guards on either side didn't even look at me. Statues in steel. I knew they knew. The entire fucking castle probably knew.

I raised my hand to knock. It shook like hell.

Once I did this, there was no crawling back. No taking it back. No forgiveness.

I closed my eyes.

All I could hear was her laugh. That loud, real, infuriating laugh. The one she hadn't given me in weeks.

Then I knocked.

The King's study smelled like incense and politics. Heavy, fake, suffocating. Sunlight bled through the stained-glass windows like a lie painted gold. King Solric stood at the far end, back turned to me, hands behind him like he was staring out at a world he still controlled.

His crown sat beside him like an afterthought.

Malakar, that smug bastard, was already seated off to the side. Legs crossed. Fingers steepled. Grinning like the spider who caught the last fly of winter.

I stood stiff. "Your Majesty. Lord Malakar."

The King didn't even turn. "You have something to confess, don't you, child?"

So, they knew.

"Yes," I said, voice tighter than I wanted.

Malakar waved a hand lazily. "Do enlighten us."

I swallowed down the bile crawling up my throat.

"Seraphina has been sneaking out of the castle at night."

No reaction.

"She rides out alone through the eastern servant's gate," I continued.

Still nothing.

"She meets with Kael."

That got them. The King turned slowly. His face was stone. His eyes were not.

"And what does she do with him?"

My voice nearly cracked. "I don't know. But she comes back looking like she's been touched by something holy. Or fucked by something she worships."

The King didn't blink. Malakar, of course, laughed softly.

"We've known," he said, like it was some damn joke. "For quite some time."

I stared at him. "What?"

"We're not idiots, Bethany," Malakar said. "You think a princess... no, a ticking political bomb can disappear that many nights and we wouldn't notice? Please. We have eyes in every corner. Spies in every shadow."

My throat dried out. "Then why... Why let me tell you?"

The King stepped forward now. His voice was gentler than I expected. "Because you chose your kingdom. That matters."

Malakar grinned wider. "And because now we have someone to blame when this all turns to shit."

The floor dropped beneath me.

I didn't remember leaving. I barely made it down the hall. My legs moved like they weren't mine. Like I was watching someone else walk in my skin.

I'd betrayed her.

I'd given her up. Handed her over. Sold her for what? Approval? Duty? Fucking peace of mind?

None of that came.

By the time I got to my room, I was shaking. My hands wouldn't stop. My teeth were clenched so tight I thought they'd shatter.

I slammed the door shut and fell onto my cot, the rough fabric scratching at my skin as I screamed into the pillow. A real, ugly, fucking scream. My ribs hurt. My throat burned. My eyes spilled tears I didn't have time to stop.

I told myself it was the right thing.

That Kael would destroy her. That she was slipping. That I was saving her from herself.

But deep down?

I knew I just threw her to the wolves and watched them lick their lips.

And worst of all?

They weren't going to eat her.

They were going to use her until there was nothing left.

And I had handed them the fucking knife.

CHAPTER XXIX
THREADS UNRAVEL

BETHANY

I've never hated silence until now.

It follows me like a ghost. Through the corridors. Into my chambers. In the halls where I used to laugh with Seraphina, where her voice used to dance off the stone. Now it's just me. Me and the fucking silence.

I avoid everyone. The guards. The maids. Even the King, though I'm sure he couldn't care less whether I live or choke on my own shame. I move like a shadow through the castle, head down, shoulders tight. If I make myself small enough, maybe I'll disappear entirely.

Seraphina hasn't been seen since she returned from her ride. That says everything. They're planning something. I can feel it in my fucking bones. And I lit the goddamn fuse.

Every hallway feels colder. Every door creaks louder. I don't eat. I barely sleep. I haven't spoken a word aloud since the King's chamber. My throat still aches from that scream I let out into my pillow, but it was nothing compared to the screams inside my fucking skull.

I pace.

I stare out windows.

I vomit guilt into the basin when I think too hard about what I've done.

I'm unraveling. Stitch by bloody stitch.

And the only person I can't outrun?

Elysandra.

I should've known she'd find me.

She always does.

I was sitting on the edge of the fountain in the inner courtyard, arms hugging my knees, trying to breathe. The garden was abandoned this early. Gray light bled into the sky, not yet dawn, and the air carried the bitter chill of an approaching storm.

And then she was just there. Like fucking smoke with a pulse.

"You look like shit," she said casually, plucking a leaf from the fountain edge and flicking it into the water.

I didn't answer.

She sat beside me without waiting for an invitation. Of course.

"How long are you planning to play the part of the palace ghost? Because you're killing the mood. Very brooding. Very dramatic. But it's starting to get old."

"Fuck off," I muttered.

Elysandra actually laughed. "There she is."

I kept my eyes on the water. My reflection looked like a stranger's—dark circles under my eyes, lips pale, skin drawn tight over too many sleepless nights.

"You knew," I said.

She hummed. "Mmhmm. About you and your late-night visit to our favorite pair of bastards? Yes."

"Then why the hell are you even talking to me?"

She tilted her head. "Because I'm curious. Watching you implode is more entertaining than the opera, frankly."

I scowled. "Go to hell."

"Already been. Found it boring."

I exhaled shakily and buried my face in my hands. "I told them everything. I gave her up."

Elysandra's voice softened. Not much. But enough.

"And now you're wondering if you've killed her."

I nodded.

"Yeah," she said. "Probably."

I didn't cry. I couldn't. The tears were gone. Burned out. All that was left was this numb, aching pit where loyalty used to live.

"I thought I was helping her," I whispered. "I thought if I just said something, it would scare her back to reality. Make her see how dangerous he is. How far she's gone."

"You thought you were saving her from herself," Elysandra said. "Classic mistake. People don't want saving. They want permission to burn."

I looked at her. "Do you ever get tired of being right?"

"No. It's delightful."

I let silence stretch. Not the choking kind from before. Just... Quiet. Still.

"So, what happens now?" I asked finally.

She gave a shrug that seemed to ripple through the air like shadows moving.

"That depends. Maybe she gets dragged through the streets and put to the axe. Maybe Kael comes back with fire in his veins. Maybe you get blamed and thrown in beside her."

I swallowed. "They said they'd handle it."

Elysandra gave me a look that made my stomach drop.

"You really think men like Malakar ever let a good scapegoat go to waste?"

My throat tightened. "They wouldn't."

She didn't answer. She didn't have to.

We sat there a while. She didn't say anything more. Just watched me fall apart in slow motion.

And when she finally stood, brushing dirt from her long coat, she said:

"You broke the thread, Bethany. Now you get to see what unravels."

Then she walked away.

Like always.

Leaving me with the truth and no one left to blame but myself.

CHAPTER XXX
The Thorn At her Throat

SERAPHINA

I t started with silence.

The kind of silence that doesn't belong in a castle. Not in Eldoria. Not in the capital, where servants scurried, and nobles gossiped, and metal boots clanged like a song written in arrogance. But when I passed the outer gates, reins slack in my fingers, the courtyard was empty.

No guards. No stable hands. No whispers.

Just silence.

It clung to the stones. It crept into my bones.

The hairs on the back of my neck rose. My horse, Hellebore, shifted nervously beneath me. Even she could smell the rot blooming beneath the stillness.

Something was wrong.

I dismounted slowly, eyes scanning every window, every alcove, every shadow. My dress clung to me, still damp with sweat and dew from the ride. The cloak I wore to conceal myself fluttered behind me like a dying flag.

I should've turned back. I should've run.

But it was too late.

They were waiting.

The moment I stepped into the main hall, the trap snapped shut.

Steel surrounded me. A dozen guards in polished black armor, shields gleaming like crows' wings, blades already drawn. They didn't shout. They didn't move. They just stood. Blocking every exit. Every breath.

At their center stood Lord Alaric.

And he was smiling.

"Welcome home, Your Highness," he said.

I stopped cold. "What is this?"

His smile didn't reach his eyes. "An intervention."

"Move."

"I'm afraid not."

I reached for the dagger hidden in my boot. Three blades instantly pointed toward my throat.

I let go.

"You are under arrest for high treason against the Crown," Alaric said, savoring every syllable.

My mouth went dry. "You're out of your godsdamn mind."

"On the contrary," he said. "I'm perfectly sane. And very well-informed."

I looked him in the eye. "You've always hated me."

"That's true. But this time, Princess, I'm not the only one. His Majesty knows. Malakar knows. The whole fucking court will know by morning."

I forced myself not to flinch. "How?"

Alaric smiled wider. "Bethany."

And just like that, the breath left my lungs.

"No," I said.

He shrugged. "She came to us. Tear-streaked, desperate. A loyal little pet who finally realized her mistress had gone feral. We never would've caught you without her."

The room spun. My knees nearly gave.

Bethany.

Bethany, who I trusted. Who I protected. Who I *loved*, gods help me, in some twisted, broken, sisterly way.

"Fuck you," I whispered.

Alaric stepped closer. "No. Fuck *you*, Princess. You were supposed to be our queen. You were supposed to be mine. Instead, you opened your legs for the enemy."

My hand moved before I thought. I slapped him across the face so hard it echoed.

The guards surged forward.

Alaric didn't stop them.

They slammed me to the ground. My head cracked against stone. My arms were yanked behind me, wrists forced into iron cuffs so tight I felt bone grind. A boot pressed between my shoulders, pinning me down.

I didn't scream.

I didn't cry.

I just stared at the floor and burned.

They dragged me through the corridors like an animal.

The halls I grew up in became a gauntlet. Every turn another face staring, another guard sneering. They didn't spit. They didn't shout. But their eyes said everything.

Whore. Traitor. Fool.

They shoved me into a cell carved from the castle's underbelly. No windows. Just mold, mildew, and stone older than blood.

Chains clinked as they locked me to the wall—a six-foot tether, just long enough to walk in a circle. Like a dog.

Alaric leaned in before the door slammed shut.

"You should start praying, Seraphina," he whispered. "You'll be kneeling again soon."

Then he left.

And I was alone.

For the first time in my life, truly, absolutely, alone.

No guards. No servants. No Bethany.

Only silence.

And the thorn at my throat, slowly pressing deeper.

CHAPTER XXXI
THE KNIFE BETWEEN US

SERAPHINA

I heard her before I saw her.

The soft tread of boots down the dungeon stairs. Hesitant. Measured. She always walked like she was trying not to be noticed. Even now. Even after what she'd done.

I sat chained to the wall, knees drawn to my chest, blood caked beneath one nostril, wrists rubbed raw where the shackles pinched my skin every time I moved. I'd lost track of time. The dark has a way of stretching seconds into hours, days into endless yawning silence.

But I knew that sound. I knew those footsteps. I knew her shadow before it even crossed the torchlight.

Bethany.

The girl I trusted more than anyone. The one I thought would ride through fire beside me.

The girl who put the knife in my back.

She stepped into the cell and froze. She looked like a ghost of herself. Pale. Eyes rimmed red, skin drawn tight over sleepless nights and gnawing guilt. Her fingers wrung themselves into knots.

She opened her mouth. Closed it. Tried again.

"Sera."

I didn't speak.

My stare did it for me.

"Please... I needed to see you."

Needed. Like I was a fix for her regret.

"You needed to see what you did?" I asked, my voice rough and dry. Like glass dragged across stone.

She winced like I slapped her. Good. Let her fucking flinch.

"I made a mistake."

"No," I said. "You made a choice. Don't you dare soften it. Don't you dare lie to both of us to make yourself feel better."

Bethany stepped forward. I stood, the chain around my ankle clinking like a death toll. My spine straightened with rage.

"I thought I was helping you," she whispered.

"Helping me?"

The laugh that came out of me was so hollow it hurt.

"You handed me over to the wolves and called it a favor. You threw me into the fucking fire and told yourself it was to keep me warm."

Her lip trembled.

"I was scared. You were disappearing into him... into Kael. You changed. You stopped talking to me. I thought he was using you."

"No," I said, stepping forward until the chain pulled tight. "You thought I stopped needing *you*. That's what this is about. Not loyalty. Not duty. *You* felt left behind."

"That's not true-"

"Isn't it?"

My voice was ice.

"You saw me happy, for the first time in years. And instead of supporting me, you ran to the same fucking men who spent their entire lives controlling me. You fed me to the same tyrants I've spent my life trying to escape."

Bethany fell to her knees.

"I'm sorry. I am so, so fucking sorry. I can't sleep. I can't think. I see your face every time I close my eyes. I was trying to protect you, and I ended up handing you over."

I wanted to cry.

I wanted to scream.

I wanted to take her hand and break it.

Instead, I turned my back.

"Whatever happens to me now, Bethany, that's on you. My blood... if it spills; it's yours to carry. Forever."

She didn't respond.

I heard her tears. I heard her breath shake.

And then I heard the door open behind her.

And close.

Leaving me alone with the ghost of the only person I ever thought I could trust.

<u>BETHANY</u>

I thought the cell would be colder.

But it wasn't the chill in the air that broke me.

It was her eyes.

I'd faced death. I'd seen men bleed out on battlefields. I'd heard mothers scream over children who wouldn't rise. I'd lived in a palace built on the bones of the forgotten.

None of that compared to the look Seraphina gave me.

Like I was already dead to her.

I tried to speak, but her silence crushed me. I reached for words. For anything.

"Sera."

My voice cracked. My throat was sandpaper and glass.

She didn't say a thing.

"Please... I needed to see you."

When she finally spoke, her voice was all blade.

"You needed to see what you did?"

Gods, I wanted to fall apart. Right there. At her feet. Like that would fix a fucking thing.

"I made a mistake," I said.

The way she looked at me, like I'd just confessed to stabbing her while she slept, made me want to vomit.

"A mistake?"

Her voice was fury made flesh.

"You made a *decision*. Don't you dare sit there and sugar-coat it. Don't you dare act like you tripped and fell into betrayal."

I stepped forward. She stood up. Even chained, she looked like a storm about to level a city.

"I thought I was helping you," I said. "I thought Kael was-"

She cut me off with a sound that wasn't quite laughter. More like a sob dressed in sarcasm.

"Helping me? You fucking *gutted* me."

And she was right.

Every word. Every syllable.

She was right.

I dropped to my knees, not to beg... but because my legs couldn't hold me anymore.

"I'm sorry," I said, choking on it. "I thought if I told them... if I said something... they'd scare you into staying. I didn't know they'd..."

She turned away.

The gesture felt like the final blow.

"Whatever happens to me now," she said quietly, "that's on you."

And she was right.

Again.

I stood on shaking legs. I wanted to touch her. To say something that might fix the bleeding thing between us.

But there was nothing.

There was no fixing it.

So, I left.

The door groaned as I opened it. It echoed behind me as it shut.

And I walked away, bleeding from a wound no one would ever see.

T.A. THORNWELL

One I'd carved into both of us with my own two fucking hands.

CHAPTER XXXII
THE SHADOW'S WAGER

SERAPHINA

T he dungeon walls were starting to whisper.

I didn't know how long I'd been down here. Time didn't exist in stone and silence. My body ached in places I hadn't known could ache, and the chain around my ankle had rubbed the skin raw. The air was damp, thick with mildew and rot, and I could taste iron on my tongue from the blood that dried beneath my lip.

I didn't sleep. I just stared. Into the dark. Into my mind.

Bethany's visit left me hollowed out. Nothing but echoes in a broken cathedral.

So, when the shadows moved in the corner of the room, I didn't flinch.

I thought I was hallucinating.

But then she spoke.

"You always looked better with a bit of blood on you. Makes your eyes sharper."

My head jerked toward the voice. She was sitting cross-legged atop an old wooden stool like she'd been there the whole time. Cloaked in black, face lit by a single flickering torch. Of course.

Elysandra.

I stared at her. "How the fuck did you get in here?"

She shrugged. "I never really left."

I swallowed hard. "If you're here to throw pity at me, save it. I've had enough of that for one lifetime."

"Pity?" She tilted her head. "Gods, no. You think I pity you? You're in chains, covered in bruises, waiting to die, and you still have the audacity to insult someone smarter than you. I admire it. Idiotic, but admirable."

I smirked. A dry, bitter ghost of a smile.

"Why are you here, then? To say goodbye? Watch me rot?"

Elysandra stood slowly, walking toward me with the grace of smoke. Her boots made no sound.

"I'm here," she said, crouching so we were eye level, "because this is the moment everything pivots. You think this is the end. It's not."

I laughed. It sounded more like a cough.

"I'm going to be executed. Publicly. Alaric made that damn clear."

Elysandra smiled. Not kindly. Not cruelly. Like someone reading the last line of a book she'd already memorized.

"Yes. You will be brought to the square. You will kneel. You will hear them read your crimes. And then... well. That depends."

I narrowed my eyes. "On what?"

She rose to her feet again and started pacing slowly.

"On fate. On fire. On men who would burn kingdoms for you."

"Kael."

She stopped. Turned.

"You think he won't come for you? After everything?"

My throat tightened.

"How do you know? How do you *know* he'll come for me?"

Elysandra smiled like the answer had always been obvious. Then she held out her hand, fingers curling into the air.

A shimmer burst to life above her palm, and shadows gathered, swirling into a vision—a ghostly window of something happening *right now.*

Bethany. On horseback. Riding like hell was behind her and heaven was ahead. Her hair whipped in the wind, face streaked with tears and determination, pushing her mount harder than I'd ever seen.

My breath caught.

Elysandra glanced at me. "Oh, I know things..."

She let the vision flicker and fade.

"Someone feels pretty guilty. And it seems as if she's going to warn someone of your fate."

Bethany.

Bethany was riding to Kael.

My throat tightened as the first real ember of hope flickered to life.

Elysandra knelt again. This time, closer.

"You don't die here, Seraphina."

Her voice dropped to a whisper, like she was saying something sacred.

"You rise here."

I swallowed. Hard.

"And if you're wrong?"

She smiled, already backing into the dark.

"Then you'll have one hell of a view from the other side."

And then she was gone.

ELYSANDRA

She looked worse than I expected.

I'd seen queens fall before. Screaming. Clawing. Crying to gods that stopped listening centuries ago. But Seraphina? She didn't scream. She didn't beg.

She sat there like a storm chained to a wall.

That kind of fury doesn't die. It waits.

I walked in without announcing myself. I didn't need to. She felt me the moment I stepped through the veil between torch-light and dark.

When she saw me, she didn't cry.

Good.

"You always looked better with a bit of blood on you. Makes your eyes sharper," I said.

She looked at me like she wasn't sure whether to throw her chain at my face or laugh.

Classic.

She asked if I pitied her.

Of course I didn't.

Pity was for people too weak to become monsters when the world demanded it.

I crouched beside her, watching the way her eyes twitched. The tremble she tried to hide in her fingers. The slight way she tilted her chin up, like defiance could protect her.

She reminded me of myself.

Before.

Before the cost of winning became too steep to keep count.

She asked how I knew Kael would come. That was the only real question. The one that mattered.

So, I showed her.

I let her see Bethany—guilt made flesh; loyalty forged in desperation. Riding toward the only man who might burn the world to keep one girl breathing.

It was enough.

The look in Seraphina's eyes changed.

I told her what she needed to hear. Not comfort. Not sympathy.

Truth.

"You don't die here. You rise here."

And I believed it.

Because the story wasn't finished. Not yet.

Bethany's knife might have cut deep, but Seraphina had always been the kind of woman who bled purpose.

Kael was coming.

The city would burn. Blood would paint the cobblestones. And from that ruin, something new would crawl from the ashes.

Maybe better. Maybe worse.

But different.

I vanished into the dark with that thought.

Let her sit with it.

Let her rage fester until it became something sharp enough to wield.

The kingdom wasn't ready.

But I was.

I'd seen this ending a hundred years ago.

And the fire was just beginning.

CHAPTER XXXII
BETHANY'S RIDE

BETHANY

T he gates slam shut behind me like a final sentence. No appeal. No reprieve. I press my heel to the mare's ribs so hard she squeals... good... and we launch into the night like a dying prayer hurled at deaf gods.

I don't feel the cold. I don't feel the wind tearing tears from my eyes. I don't feel the raw burn in my throat when I swallow down the bile that wants to rise every time Seraphina's face flickers behind my eyes.

She didn't scream. She didn't curse me. That would've been mercy. She just looked. Like I was a rotting carcass she'd stumbled across in the road. Something you step around, so the stink doesn't cling to your boots.

You deserve worse, I tell myself. The hooves pound the frozen earth. My bones rattle in my skin. I want them to break. I want to feel them splinter like my world did.

If there was a blade in my belt, I'd have slit my own throat already... but Kael has to know first. I owe Seraphina *that*. I owe her my blood, but she'll have to settle for the only thing I have left to give: a warning.

The trees rush past, skeletal arms clawing at my cloak, my hair, my face. They can have it all. Let them strip me to bone and regret. I won't stop. I won't flinch.

I betrayed her. Over and over the words hammer the inside of my skull. I taste iron... I bit my tongue, I think. Good. Bleed. Bleed for every lie that dripped sweet and poisoned from your mouth.

I lean forward, nose buried in the mare's sweaty mane. *Don't die on me now.* She's panting like she's got a dagger in her lung... same as me. I've been dead since the moment Seraphina's eyes turned to ice. This ride is just the last twitch of the corpse.

I should've stayed. Should've let them hang me beside her. But no... I had to believe there was a scrap of redemption left to claw at. So here I am. Beaten hooves and broken promises pounding through the dark.

No fear. Fear would be kindness. Fear says you've got something left to lose. I don't. There's no life waiting for me when the sun comes up. I'm already ash.

The wind howls through my ribs like a church bell tolling for the dead. *For me.* I lean into it, dare it to split me open. I deserve the cold. The dark. The emptiness.

Kael. Kael. Kael.

His name beats in time with the mare's dying gallop. If he kills me when I get there... good. Maybe his sword can carve the stain off my soul that my own hands were too soft to cut away.

I see the fires. Flickering in the trees like a promise I don't deserve. Kael's men. Kael's last chance. Seraphina's last breath hanging by the torn thread of my spine.

I ram my heels into the mare one final time; she screams beneath me but obeys. We crash through the line of guards, curses and torches whipping past.

Kael's tent looms. I don't bother slowing. I throw myself off the saddle while the mare's still moving. The world tilts, my shoulder hits dirt, I taste blood, or mud, or both.

I crawl. Hands clawing earth, knees split open on frozen roots. The tent flap... rough canvas rips against my raw knuckles.

He's there. Kael. War map. Fury eyes. His mouth parts... my name, maybe.

"Kael—" It tears out of me like a dying animal. I see his shadow lunge forward.

I want to tell him. I want to spit the truth into the fire before I choke on it forever. But the blackness surges up, sweet and heavy. My mouth opens...

Nothing.

I drop. Knees first, then face, dirt in my teeth. My last thought is a wish... that the cold will keep me down. That the silence will bury me deep enough Seraphina never has to see my wretched ghost haunting her final dawn.

Darkness.

CHAPTER XXXIII

THE MONSTER IN THE MIRROR

SERAPHINA

T he door creaked.

And I knew.

I didn't need to see his face. I didn't need the light of the torch to confirm what my skin already knew. The air changed when he walked in. It got thicker, more suffocating, like the walls were suddenly too close and the room had no air left to breathe.

Alaric.

His boots echoed on the stone like mockery.

He was alone. That was the part that made my stomach twist. The guards didn't come with him this time. No witness. No buffer. No one to stop him if he decided today was the day he broke something just to see how it screamed.

I stood slowly, chains clinking as I moved. I squared my shoulders despite the bruises, despite the ripped remains of my dignity.

He shut the door behind him with a deliberate slowness that made my skin crawl.

"Look at you," he said, voice low and coiled. "Still proud. Still trying to pretend you haven't been brought to heel."

I met his gaze with fire.

"Get. Out."

He laughed. Not a hearty laugh. Not even a bitter one. It was the kind of laugh men make when they think they've already won.

"You could've had it all," he said, circling me like a jackal. "A throne. A kingdom. Me."

"I'd rather be buried in a ditch with rats chewing my bones than have you inside me."

His jaw twitched.

"But instead, you gave yourself to him. To that filthy dog from Morvath."

He stepped closer.

"Did he make you scream? Did he mark you with his hands?"

I didn't respond. That made it worse. He needed an answer. Needed me to validate his insecurities.

I just stared.

That silence cut deeper than anything I could've said.

His face cracked.

"He used you. You were nothing but a hole to him."

I smiled. Slow. Poisoned.

"And I begged him to use me again."

He snapped.

He lunged, slamming me against the wall. The chain above me jerked taut as he pinned my wrists. His other hand went to my throat, not tight, not yet, just pressing, enough to show me who he wanted to be.

His breath reeked of wine and something sour, like rotting ambition.

"I could take you right now," he hissed. "I could make you mine. Make you forget him."

I didn't blink.

"You could try."

He snarled and reached for the torn fabric of my dress.

That was it.

I snapped.

I surged up, slammed my knee between his legs with everything I had left. He howled, buckled, and I wrapped the length of chain around his neck before he hit the floor.

"You wanted me, Alaric?"

I yanked hard. He choked, clawed, thrashed beneath me.

"This is what you get. This is all of me."

I leaned down, voice low, venomous.

"Kael fucked me until I couldn't breathe. Until I forgot my name. Seven times, Alaric. Seven."

He gurgled, face turning a beautiful shade of purple.

"And when I watched his eyes while he was inside me, I thanked the gods I was never yours."

The door crashed open.

Steel clanged. Boots thundered. Arms grabbed me, tore me back, fists striking, knuckles splitting my lip. I didn't scream.

They pinned me to the wall like a beast.

Alaric coughed on the floor, crawling like the worm he was.

I spat blood and looked up at the guards, eyes wild, voice steady.

"You're all going to die."

The room froze.

"Each and every one of you," I said through clenched teeth. "When the gates fall. When fire rains. I will walk these halls in your blood."

The youngest guard flinched.

Good.

"And when I'm done," I whispered, "I'll spit on your corpses."

No one said a word.

Not even Alaric.

Because somewhere inside all of them, even him... They knew I wasn't lying.

CHAPTER XXXIV
THE EXECUTIONER'S WALK

SERAPHINA

It began before dawn. The darkness hadn't yet lifted, and the cold had teeth that bit through the thin remains of my tattered dress. I sat curled against the damp stone wall, arms hugging my knees, chains slack but never far enough to forget. I hadn't slept. Not really. My eyes had closed, but the nightmares stayed. They never needed sleep, only silence.

Then came the boots.

Heavy. Rhythmic. Final.

The iron door groaned open, and the world changed.

Torchlight bled through the threshold, flickering off the damp stones like blood on water. Shadows moved behind it, three, maybe four. I couldn't tell. I barely breathed. My body ached like it had grown old overnight, like I had lived a century in a single cell.

The guards stepped in. Black-clad. Helmets pulled low over their eyes, not to protect themselves, but to spare them the guilt of looking at the woman they were about to walk to her death. One of them moved toward me, and I stood before he could touch me. Pride. My only shield.

No words were exchanged. Just the rattle of keys, the metallic kiss of unlocking chains, and then hands on my arms. Not rough. Not gentle. Just final.

They bound my wrists behind my back.

Then the collar.

It was a tradition. A rusted iron collar clamped around the neck of traitors. Not prisoners. Not criminals.

Traitors.

The man behind me clipped the leash to it.

And they pulled.

The walk from the dungeon to the courtyard was longer than I remembered. Every echo of our steps sounded like a heartbeat I couldn't claim. My own was buried too deep in fear. The walls seemed to lean inward, watching. Judging. I wanted to scream, to run, to vanish.

Instead, I walked.

Because they made me.

Because there was no other way left to go.

When we reached the outer gates of the castle, I saw the crowd.

And the sound hit me like a fist.

They were chanting. Screaming. Spitting. The roar of them was alive, savage, desperate for a spectacle. For blood. For mine.

"Whore!"

"Death to the traitor!"

"Let her rot in hell!"

The first piece of food hit my shoulder. A cabbage, rotten and wet. It slid down my arm like a stain. Then another. And another. Tomatoes. Apples. A rock. Spit. Everywhere. On my legs. My face. My hair. It clung to me, warm and vile, like shame given form.

I kept walking.

My ankles were shackled, and the leash pulled against my throat every time I hesitated. My feet moved like they belonged to someone else. I wasn't Seraphina anymore. I wasn't royalty. I wasn't human.

I was a thing being paraded through the street.

The crowd pressed in from both sides. Faces blurred together in a sea of hatred. Children held up by parents, their tiny fingers pointing. Elders with rotten vegetables in their hands. Nobles in windows with goblets raised like they were toasting the end of a war.

And it was a war.

Me against the world.

The execution square came into view, framed by stone arches and black banners.

The platform loomed in the center like an altar to cruelty. Wood stained darker by decades of blood. Chains embedded into the frame. The block itself, scarred and soaked in history, waited like a mouth ready to consume.

The executioner stood beside it, tall, faceless beneath a leather hood. He tested the blade, slow and showy, dragging it across a whetstone. Sparks flickered. The sound was bone deep.

I stared at the block.

And I scanned the crowd.

The walls.

The gates.

The rooftops.

Nothing.

No Kael.

No rescue.

No shadows to hide in. No arrows. No miracle.

Just eyes. Hundreds of eyes. Waiting for the axe to fall.

I was shoved up the stairs.

Each step sounded like a drumbeat in a funeral march.

Wood creaked beneath my bare feet. The air was colder up here. The wind sharper. Or maybe it just felt that way because of what was coming.

They placed me at the center.

I saw her.

Elysandra.

Standing on a rooftop above the crowd. Her cloak billowed like wings. Her face was still. Unreadable.

Our eyes locked.

She didn't smile.

She mouthed the words:

Long live the Queen.

Then the hood came down.

Darkness swallowed me.

The crowd grew louder. My breathing was loud in my own ears, ragged, uneven. My knees shook beneath me.

Then I heard his voice.

Alaric.

That oily tone, too pleased with itself. Too loud. Too triumphant.

"By order of King Solric and Lord Malakar, under decree of the Crown of Eldoria, the traitor Seraphina is hereby sentenced to death."

The crowd cheered.

"For the crime of high treason. For consorting with the enemy. For betraying her people and her bloodline."

He paused, let the silence build.

"Let this be the fate of all who would shame the throne."

And I accepted it.

The hope I'd clung to for days died in that moment.

No footsteps. No rescue.

Kael wasn't coming.

The weight of it hollowed me out. My chest felt like a cave. My mouth was dry. My eyes burned beneath the hood.

I was no longer afraid.

I was nothing.

They pushed me to my knees.

The wood was rough against my skin. Splinters bit into my legs. My collar was unclipped. My arms pulled forward, shackled to the front of the block. The crowd's cheers turned rhythmic, chanting for blood, for vengeance, for an end.

The executioner stepped forward.

I heard the axe lift.

I closed my eyes.

And I laid my head down.

The world narrowed to one sound:

Breath.

Mine.

Theirs.

And the weight of the blade in the air.

I was ready.

Let it end.

Let them remember me for what I was:

Not a traitor.

But a warning.

CHAPTER XXXV
KAEL'S RECKONING

KAEL

T he crowd was a fucking riot of rot and sound.

They howled like starving wolves, spit flying, hands clutching spoiled fruit and rocks and whatever else they could throw. Every face twisted with the kind of righteous rage that only cowards wear when they know the victim's already bleeding.

And they wanted her dead.

Seraphina.

I was in the back, hood pulled low, bow slung across my back, heart thundering so loud I was sure someone would hear it and turn. But no one did. They were too busy baying for blood. *Her* blood.

Bethany's voice still echoed in my ears from hours ago. Frantic. Shaking. "They're going to kill her. Today. You have to come. You have to, *please.*"

She led us here. Whispered secrets through clenched teeth, hands stained with guilt and desperation. She didn't ask for forgiveness. She knew she didn't deserve it.

And I didn't offer it. But I followed her.

Thirty shield brothers. My finest. We moved through old tunnels slick with rot and silence, breathing the air of the dead just to reach the surface alive.

We emerged under a city on fire with hate.

And now we waited.

Scattered in the crowd.

Weapons hidden. Eyes locked on the platform.

On *her*.

When they dragged her out, something in me turned to ash.

Her dress, what was left of it, hung in strips. One sleeve torn clean off. The bruises across her collarbone bloomed like ink. Her ankles were scraped raw from the shackles. Her hair was wild, tangled, still crusted with dirt and dried blood.

But her spine?

Straight as a fucking blade.

They pushed her forward, and she walked. Chin lifted. Face stone.

The kind of strength that shouldn't exist.

Not after what they'd done.

Not after they tried to erase her.

But she walked anyway.

And I...

I wanted to burn the world.

She didn't see me.

Not yet.

She scanned the rooftops. The crowd. The horizon. Every desperate glance was another needle jammed beneath my ribs.

She was still hoping.

Still believing I might come.

And every passing second killed her a little more.

Alaric stood center stage, voice booming. His words were a spit-polished death sentence.

"Seraphina of Eldoria, you stand accused of high treason against the crown..."

I tuned the rest out. I didn't need to hear it. I could *see* it.

The way she flinched when he said her name.

The way her eyes dulled as the decree was read.

The way her gaze stopped searching the horizon.

Like hope had finally given up.

The executioner stepped forward

Big bastard. Axe already in hand. The blade was stained. Used. He twirled it like it was an extension of his arm. A showman. A killer who liked his job too much.

Seraphina didn't cry.

Didn't beg.

She just... knelt.

The guards forced her down, boots against her back, fists gripping her arms. Her knees hit the wood with a *crack* that echoed across the square. The sound went through me like a blade.

Then came the hood.

And my breath caught.

One last glance. One last look.

That's when she saw her.

Elysandra.

Standing above the crowd, cloaked in black, arms folded. No one else noticed her. Of course they didn't.

But Seraphina did.

Their eyes locked.

Elysandra mouthed four words.

"Long live the queen."

Then the hood came down.

And Seraphina's world went black.

My arrow was already nocked.

I drew the bowstring to my cheek.

The world narrowed to a single breath.

The executioner raised his axe.

And I let the arrow fly.

It punched through the air with a hiss.

Buried itself right between his eyes.

He didn't scream. Didn't even blink.

Just dropped like a puppet with its strings cut, the axe tumbling from his grip and thudding beside Seraphina's head.

The crowd gasped, then chaos erupted.

My men moved first.

Exploding from the crowd, cloaks thrown aside, steel flashing like lightning. They didn't speak. They didn't shout.

They just killed.

Guards. Soldiers. Anyone who stood in their way.

Blood hit the cobblestones before people realized what the fuck was happening.

I shoved through bodies, people screaming, trampling each other to flee. I didn't care. I was already moving.

I tore through the chaos, dodging stalls and corpses and shrieking nobles. Someone tried to grab me, I put a knife through his throat without breaking stride.

The main gate loomed ahead.

Two guards blocked it. One reached for his horn.

He never got the chance.

I drove a dagger through his chest, ripped it free, then spun and slammed the other into the wall, blade to his throat.

He begged.

I didn't listen.

The gate's locking mechanism was rusted, old as sin. But I'd studied it. Knew what to do.

I threw my weight into the lever. It groaned. Chains screeched. The counterweights dropped.

And the gate began to rise.

Slow.

Loud.

But it *rose*.

And beyond it... my army.

Alistair at the front. Morvath's banners high. His sword already slick with blood.

They poured through like a tide of vengeance.

And Eldoria would drown.

I turned and ran.

Back to the square.

Back to the stage.

Back to *her*.

Seraphina was still there.

Still kneeling.

Frozen.

The guards were confused, half-dead, scattered, screaming into the din. One reached for her. My arrow caught him in the neck.

I vaulted the steps two at a time.

Ripped the hood from her head.

And saw her eyes.

Wide.

Tears.

Disbelief.

Relief.

"Kael," she breathed.

Not a question.

Just... *everything*.

I cut her free.

She collapsed into me, shaking like the earth before the break.

I held her tight.

"You're not dying today," I said.

She didn't answer.

She didn't need to.

She just clung to me.

And behind us?

The kingdom burned.

CHAPTER XXXVI

A SYMPHONY OF CHAOS

ELYSANDRA

T hey marched her like a lamb dressed for slaughter. however, the dress itself was barely still on her.

I watched from my perch atop the eastern facade of the old temple. Cracked stone beneath me, wind tugging at my cloak, the scent of iron and rot wafting from the square below like perfume at a funeral.

And gods, what a *beautiful* fucking funeral this was.

Seraphina. My star pupil. My shattered little phoenix.

Dragged in chains through the same streets where they once kissed the hem of her gowns.

Now they spit on her.

Called her whore.

Traitor.

Monster.

I smiled.

Not out of cruelty.

But out of satisfaction.

Because every insult, every rock, every tomato that exploded against her bare shoulder was another line of music in the symphony I'd been composing for *decades*.

I didn't blink as she stumbled. Didn't flinch when the guards shoved her up the stairs like she was livestock.

They thought they'd won.

They thought they were finally caging the storm.

But storms aren't caged.

They're *called*.

And this one? I called it *years* ago.

Malakar had tried to throw things off course, of course.

He sniffed around places I had left intentionally cracked. Sent his little shadows after Seraphina. Followed her. Hunted her.

He fancied himself clever.

He fancied himself a player in my game.

Nothing more than a little *bitch*, a pawn I move on my chessboard.

But Malakar never saw the strings he danced on. Never noticed the blade I hung above him like a chandelier in a lightning storm.

And now?

He'd watch his kingdom crumble.

Because of me.

Because of *her*.

Because I told the threads where to pull.

From up here, I saw everything.

Alaric, puffed up and venom-drunk, reading the charges with the dramatic flair of a man who thought this day would make him matter.

The crowd, their eyes wide, mouths snarling, mouths open, hungry for blood they didn't earn.

And her.

Seraphina.

Kneeling.

Proud and trembling and beautiful and broken all at once.

I saw the way her eyes flicked to the rooftops.

Desperation, raw, shaking, swallowing the last drops of hope like poison.

And then she saw me.

I stepped forward, out of the shadow, just enough for her to see.

Our eyes met through the veil of despair.

And I mouthed it slowly, deliberately, with all the gravity of prophecy:

"Long live the queen."

Then the hood came down.

I leaned back against the stone and exhaled slowly, savoring the pause in the music.

Just one more beat.

Just one more...

Thwap.

The arrow whistled through the square like a kiss of death.

And the executioner?

Dropped like a sack of meat with a metal hat.

I grinned.

Right on cue.

Chaos detonated.

My chaos.

Kael's men erupted from the crowd like roaches with blades. Civilians screamed, shoved, trampled each other trying to escape a war they didn't see coming.

Fires. Screams. Steel in the sun.

It was orgasmic.

Kael burst through the side streets, carving through soldiers like a wolf among chickens, and I watched him hit the gate lever with the desperation of a man running out of time.

The gate groaned open, and the army poured in like a second wave of blood.

I whispered to the wind: "Curtain's up."

And gods, what a show.

He reached her.

Right as I'd seen it.

Tore the hood off.

Held her like salvation incarnate.

Their eyes met, and I felt it, like lightning in my bones.

The moment the world changed shape.

The moment death was denied.

And destiny was fed a new name.

My grin faded just slightly as I scanned the rooftops.

Something... *off*.

A piece missing from the puzzle.

Bethany.

Where the fuck was Bethany?

She should've been here. At the edge of the stage. Eyes wide. Watching what her betrayal had bought.

But she wasn't.

Which meant one of two things.

Either she was dead...

Or she was *still in play*.

And I do so love surprises.

I stepped back into the shadows.

The screams echoed below. The banners of Morvath flew high. The smell of smoke and blood and burning ambition filled my lungs.

My web had never been tighter.

And the queen?

Oh, she was almost ready to reign.

But first...

Let the kingdom bleed.

Let the fire spread.

Let the monsters finish what the saints started.

Because this?

This wasn't the end of the world.

It was the beginning of hers.

CHAPTER XXXVII

THE CROWN AND THE CORPSE

SERAPHINA

I don't remember the first scream.

Just the blood.

The square had turned into a killing floor, fire cracking through the bones of the city, steel singing death songs in the wind, men dying like animals. Kael's shield brothers were cutting through Eldorian soldiers like reapers let loose from myth.

And in the middle of it all, he held my hand.

Kael.

Warm. Solid. Moving like a god carved from war itself.

I couldn't breathe.

Couldn't blink.

Couldn't do anything except let him drag me through the chaos, his hand locked around mine like an anchor as the world went to hell.

Everywhere I looked, something died.

A man's throat opened three feet from me, arterial spray painting my shoulder as he collapsed. A woman screamed for her child just before a blade tore through her back. The air was thick with smoke, ash, and the reek of piss-soaked fear.

Kael didn't falter.

Every soldier who came near us didn't last more than three seconds. His sword was an extension of his fury, and that fury had a name... it was *mine*.

"Stay behind me," he shouted over the chaos. "Keep low!"

I nodded, not trusting my voice. My legs felt like they were made of glass. Every heartbeat was a hammer in my chest.

But I kept moving.

Because he pulled me forward.

Because he still believed there was a way out.

We ducked into an alley, two turns off the execution square, bodies still hitting the cobblestones behind us. The sound of fire consuming the merchant stalls crackled like applause. My throat burned with smoke. The cold of the dungeon was still on my skin.

Kael paused.

He looked at me... really looked at me, for the first time since the arrow had flown.

I saw it in his eyes then.

The storm. The *love*.

He dropped his sword for just a breath. Took my face in both hands.

His palms were slick with blood.

"I didn't come to save a crown," he said, voice ragged. "I came to save *you*."

I blinked, tears spilling instantly, uninvited.

He leaned in, pressing his forehead to mine, his breath warm despite the cold iron tang of death all around us.

"I should've told you before," he whispered. "Back in the ruins. Back in the woods. Every damn night I held you."

I clutched his wrists, breath hitching.

"Tell me now."

He smiled. Gods, even now, *he smiled.*

"I would've set the world on fire for one more minute with you."

Then he kissed me.

And for just a moment, just a *moment...* there was no war.

Just him.

Just us.

Just breath and lips and the quiet hum of a future we might still steal.

And then it happened.

That future ended.

A blade tore through Kael's back, steel ripping through skin, bone, and heart.

I felt the spray of his blood hit my cheek before I heard him gasp.

Then he jerked, the warmth draining from his mouth as it left mine, eyes wide in a confusion that would haunt me for the rest of my life.

He stumbled back into me, falling like the world itself had cracked under him.

The blade protruded from his chest.

His blood poured down my front like a second skin.

"*No...*"

I caught him as he fell.

And standing behind him, sword slick and face twisted in triumph, was *Alaric.*

The coward.

The would-be king.

The piece of shit who'd wanted to rule beside me and couldn't even hold a sword on the frontlines.

He grinned; teeth pink with effort.

"Funny," he said. "He dies first."

Then he turned his eyes on me.

Still holding the sword.

Still dripping with *Kael's* blood.

"You'll thank me for this one day, Seraphina."

Something broke.

Inside me.

A dam. A lock. A tether. I don't know.

But it *snapped*.

Time slowed. My ears rang. My breath went shallow. My vision blurred, and the only thing I could see clearly was his sword... Kael's sword, lying in the blood beside me.

I reached for it.

I didn't speak.

I didn't scream.

I just *moved*.

He never expected it.

He never saw the fury coming.

The moment I grabbed Kael's blade; I was no longer a prisoner. No longer a princess. No longer a pawn.

I was *death*.

I plunged the sword into Alaric's thigh, twisting it until I felt the bone splinter. He howled, collapsing forward, swinging wildly.

I didn't let him rise.

I grabbed a dagger from his own belt and drove it into his shoulder... deep, to the hilt, then kicked him flat on his back.

"Wait," he gasped.

I didn't.

I stabbed him in the gut. Once. Twice. A third time.

He gurgled something pathetic, spit mixing with blood.

"You touched me," I whispered. "You *killed him.*"

And then I *tore* into him.

Kael's blade took his left hand clean off.

He screamed until I rammed the sword through his open mouth, splitting his skull with a sound I'll never forget.

Still, it wasn't enough.

I dragged the blade down his chest, spilling his insides across the ground, gore and bile steaming in the cool air. I carved until my arms ached. Until there was nothing left but ruin.

Only then did I stop.

I turned.

Kael was on his side, coughing, blood bubbling from his lips, staining his teeth. His eyes were glassy now. Dimming.

I dropped the sword and crawled to him, knees scraping through blood and bone. I cradled his head in my lap, sobbing, hands shaking so hard I could barely keep him still.

"Don't," I whispered. "Don't you dare."

He smiled again—*gods, how could he still smile?*

He coughed, groaned.

"I'm not... gonna make it."

"No," I shook my head violently. "No, you don't get to say that. You don't get to..."

"Shh..."

His hand found mine. Weak. Cold.

"You're the Queen now. You always were."

"Kael, please..."

He squeezed.

"Alistair... he'll stand beside you. He'll help you rebuild. He swore it to me."

Tears poured down my face, hot against my cheek.

"I don't want Alistair. I want *you*."

"I know," he whispered.

And then, voice so soft I almost missed it:

"I never knew peace... until I saw you smile."

I choked on a sob.

"I love you."

"I love you too," he said.

Then he inhaled, once. Shaky.

And exhaled.

And never breathed again.

I didn't scream.

I *howled*.

A sound ripped from my chest that wasn't human. A scream so primal it cut through the clash of battle, rose over the rooftops, and shattered the bones of the sky itself.

Everyone heard it.

Morvath.

Eldoria.

The dying.

The victorious.

T.A. THORNWELL

And they knew.

The Queen had risen.

And she was made of blood.

CHAPTER XXXVIII
BLOOD FOR A KINGDOM

K ael's blood still stains my hands.

It's dry now... cracked into my skin like a second set of veins, threading his death into mine. I haven't washed it off. Won't. Not until I've given every drop back.

His sword is a natural extension of my arm. The dagger, his dagger, rests against my thigh... warm, ready. I drew them both when I carved Alaric open. I haven't let go since.

This kingdom took him from me.

So, I'll take the kingdom.

One corpse at a time.

I barrel through the smoke and screams, slicing through soldiers and innocents alike. There is no difference anymore. Not to me. If they stand in my path, they fall. If they scream, I scream louder. If they bleed... gods help them, I drink it in like wine.

And then...

I see him.

Standing at the edge of the firelight. Not moving. Just watching.

Kael.

Not as he died... broken, pale, bleeding out in my arms, but as he was before all this: tall, armor cracked from war, eyes fierce with purpose. The inferno flickers through him like he's made of smoke and memory.

I blink.

He's still there.

"Kael," I whisper, low and hoarse and dangerous.

His lips curl into the faintest, most haunting smile.

"Burn it all, my love," he says. His voice is inside me, inside my chest, my spine, my skull. *"Leave nothing for them to rule."*

I tear my blade through a soldier's throat so fast his body doesn't know it's dead yet. It just... crumples. Behind me, fire devours tapestries older than I am. Blood coats the marble like warpaint.

Kael's ghost... vision... hallucination... floats beside me. Silent steps. Watching me work.

"Do not flinch," he murmurs as I gut a man screaming for his mother. *"Do not stop."*

I don't.

A flash of steel, Kael's dagger in my hand now, not the sword. It's faster, meaner. I slam it into a guard's side, pull it out and slice his throat with the same motion. My arms are aching. My muscles scream. But I keep going. I *have* to.

"Are you real?" I ask the ghost. My voice cracks.

Kael only tilts his head. His blue eyes... Kael's eyes, glow like frost beneath firelight.

"Does it matter?" he says. *"I'm here, and they're dying."*

Another soldier tries to run. I don't give him the luxury. I grab him by the back of the neck and drag him to the ground. I bring Kael's sword down like judgment... again, and again, and *again...* until there's nothing left but wet noise.

"That's it," Kael says. *"That's my girl... That's my Queen."*

Is he a ghost?

A fracture in my mind?

Or has my grief summoned him from the Otherworld to witness my rage?

I don't know. I don't care. He's here. And that's enough.

Smoke thickens. Banners fall. The Eldorian crest... my family's crest, catches fire and turns to ash above me.

"What do you see?" he asks.

I stare at the flames as they climb higher, devouring history.

"I see the end."

"No," he whispers. *"You see the beginning."*

I push forward, Kael at my side like a shadow that refuses to leave. No one else seems to see him. Alistair rushes in from behind, breath ragged.

"Seraphina! We need to get to the throne room!"

I don't look away from the burning crest.

"I *am* the throne," I say flatly, then I turn to him with blood in my eyes. "Let's finish this."

Alistair doesn't ask questions.

We move together now, but my mind isn't here. It's split, half in the battle, half in the beyond. Kael follows. Always Kael. His voice lingers over my shoulder as I cut through the last of the king's loyalists.

"No mercy. No forgiveness... No gods but us."

By the time we reach the throne room, I'm soaked in blood. Not metaphorically. Literally. My dress clings to me like a second skin of ruin. My breath comes in growls.

The door opens.

And the last bastard left in this rotting kingdom will die screaming.

CHAPTER XXXIX
THE THRONE BLEEDS

T he door creaks open on rusted hinges, groaning like it knows what's coming.

The throne room smells like fear. And piss. Cowardice has a scent, sour, sharp, bitter. My boots squish against the blood-soaked carpet, leaving red footprints on royal silk. The windows are shattered. Smoke curls in like ghost fingers. Everything the king once ruled is burning to ash just outside these walls.

And he's cowering on the fucking throne.

The man who condemned me, his daughter... to die like a dog in the dirt, is now clutching the arms of his gilded seat like it's a lifeline. His crown is crooked. His face pale. His eyes... once full of sermons and speeches, now wide with dread.

Good.

Kael's sword drips with death in my hand. His dagger, slick with blood, rests warm at my hip. I can still feel Kael's heartbeat in the hilt. Or maybe it's mine. Who the fuck knows anymore.

Alistair moves beside me like a shadow, silent and watchful. But it's *Kael's* ghost I'm listening to.

He stands just to my right, always to my right... even in death, expression unreadable. Cold, brutal, beautiful.

I pause ten paces from the throne and glance at him. No one else can see. They'd say I'm staring at nothing.

"Well?" I ask him.

Kael tilts his head. Blue eyes like frostbite.

"Do it."

I nod once.

Then I step forward.

The king raises a hand. Pathetic. Trembling. "Seraphina... please. We can—"

"*Don't.*" My voice is gravel and rot. "Don't you fucking dare try to beg."

"You don't understand..."

I raise Kael's blade and point it at his chest. "No, *you* don't understand. You sentenced me to death because I loved a man you couldn't control. You strung me up like a traitor for following my heart. And now? Now you're hiding on your fucking throne while your kingdom BURNS."

I stalk forward. One step. Another.

"I *am* your legacy, father. I am the consequence of your cowardice. You made me into this. You *forged* me in your betrayal."

I stop at the base of the steps.

"Say his name," I whisper. "Say Kael's name before you die."

The king's lips tremble, but nothing comes out.

I look to Kael again.

"He's not worth words," Kael murmurs. *"Just blood."*

I take the first step up.

"He begged for peace."

Another step.

"He offered mercy."

Another.

"And you killed him for it."

I'm face-to-face with the king now. My father. The man I once loved. Once idolized. Now just a quivering bag of skin and guilt.

I drop Kael's sword.

He blinks, stunned. Stupid.

Then I draw the dagger.

Kael's dagger.

"Thrones aren't built on blood," I whisper, "but they bleed for it."

And I *stab*.

The blade sinks into his gut. He gasps like a fish pulled from water. I twist. Pull. Stab again. And again. And *again*.

Screaming. Squelching. Wet, ragged gasps.

Kael stands at my shoulder, watching.

I look to him.

"Is it enough?"

He says nothing.

I stab again.

"Now is it enough?"

T.A. THORNWELL

Still nothing.

My arm moves on instinct, rage, memory. I'm not just killing a king. I'm killing the past. The lies. The pain.

Finally, Kael whispers.

"Now."

I step back.

The king slumps in the throne like discarded meat. Blood pours down the steps in rivers. The crown clatters to the ground, rolling like a severed head. It bumps against my boot. I kick it away. His body hangs in the throne for a few moments and then slides onto the floor.

Smoke pours in from the broken windows.

Outside, Eldoria's banners fall from the towers, set ablaze mid-air. Crimson and gold consumed by black fire.

In their place, the black sigil of Morvath rises.

One kingdom dies. Another takes its place.

"And now?" I ask Kael. "What now?"

He turns to me. Smiles small, sad, proud.

"Take it."

I walk to the throne... his blood still warm on it and sit.

Kael's sword rests across my knees. The dagger still in my hand. The crown stays on the floor where it belongs.

Alistair approaches slowly. He looks at me like I'm something not quite human anymore. Maybe I'm not.

He kneels.

"I swore to Kael," he says quietly. "And now I swear to you. Not because I want power. Not for glory. But because he trusted you. And because I do, too."

I stare at him. My voice is hoarse when it comes. "This won't be a marriage built on love."

"I know," he says. "I know your heart doesn't belong to me. It never will."

Silence.

"I don't need your heart, Seraphina. I need your strength. And you need someone who will *never* try to replace what you lost."

He lifts his eyes.

"I know I'm not... and never will be... *your* King. But I will be the King who rules at your side. And I will *never* try to replace *your* King... because he was *my* King too."

Something inside me breaks all over again.

I glance to my right. Kael's ghost is still there.

He nods once.

And I breathe.

CHAPTER XL
SMOKE, ASH, AND BANNERS

ELYSANDRA

From atop the parapets, the kingdom looks like a dying star. Red. Orange. Black. Smoke rolls thick through the ruins like the breath of some ancient god come to swallow it whole. And I... faithful little harbinger, stand and watch the end as it's written.

The banners fall first. Always the banners.

Crimson and gold, Eldoria's proud sigil, catches fire before it even hits the ground. It flutters like a dying bird, curls in on itself, and becomes ash before it can land. A fitting metaphor. The old world doesn't get to die with dignity.

In its place rises the obsidian banner of Morvath. Sharper. Colder. Truer.

I press one gloved hand to the stone ledge, letting my fingers feel the vibrations. War is still alive beneath me... a beast with too many teeth and too much pride to just lay down and die cleanly.

I can feel every scream, every sob, every sword buried in bone.

And gods, it's *beautiful*.

Not in the way soft-hearted fools write poems about. No, this is the beauty of inevitability. Of justice that doesn't beg for permission. Of fate fulfilled, sharp and absolute.

"She's done it," I whisper to no one. *"She's truly done it."*

Seraphina... blood-soaked and burning with vengeance, has carved her name into the kingdom's spine. I felt the moment her blade pierced the king's flesh like a tremor through my bones. His life force evaporated like steam off scorched stone, leaving behind nothing but the rot he built his legacy on.

She sits the throne now. She wears no crown... she *is* the crown. The kingdom doesn't need gold to know who owns it. It needs blood. And she gave more than enough.

Somewhere down below, Alistair stands beside her. Loyal. Steady. The wrong King... but the right sword.

And Malakar?

He fled.

That rat bastard took one look at the fires and the fury and decided his survival outweighed his loyalty. Typical. He always was more shadow than man. No final words. No duel. No honor. Just the fading echo of his footsteps disappearing into the northern pass like smoke.

Coward.

But that's fine.

"He has his day coming," I murmur to the ash-thick air. *"I've seen it."*

And when it comes, I hope he hears the screams of the dying as clearly as I do now.

Because *I* hear them all.

You think it's just steel and flame that marks the end of a kingdom?

No. I feel them.

Every soul that slips from this realm tonight whispers across my skin like wind. Their ends were woven long ago, and I, the unwilling weaver, have carried them like weights around my neck. I feel their pain. Their fury. Their relief. Most pass like embers, expected. Accounted for. A ledger finally paid.

But...

There was one I didn't see.

A soul not written in the bones. A death I *did not predict.*

And it haunts me.

Even now, with ash painting the sky and the prophecy fulfilled, it lingers in my chest like a splinter. One too many threads were cut, and I can't tell whose.

That... is disturbing.

Because I've known every ending. I've felt them all.

But this?

This one was *wrong.*

Below, the final fires are dwindling. Not dying... transforming.

Eldoria isn't ending. Not truly. Kingdoms never *end.* They simply change shape. And this new shape? It's feral. Ruthless. Reborn in blood and blade and rage.

A woman sits the throne. A ghost whispers in her ear. And I watch it all unfold like I've done a thousand times before.

This was never my plan. Not in the way mortals think.

I made no bargains to bring this about. I cast no great spell to ensure the outcome. Fate isn't so easily manipulated... it doesn't barter. It demands.

And I?

I am not the author.

I am the *harbinger*.

And fate's will is done.

For now...

CHAPTER XLI
ASH-STAINED SILENCE

SERAPHINA

I don't know what brought me here.

Maybe it was muscle memory, maybe grief. Or maybe I was just looking for something that still felt like mine in the ruins of this fucking kingdom. Either way, my boots dragged me through the charred remnants of the castle halls until I stood before the door, I swore I'd never walk through again.

My old quarters.

Princess Seraphina's gilded cage.

The doorknob was cold, spiteful in my hand. The hinges screamed as it creaked open. And that's when the world stopped.

I didn't notice the room at first. Not the golden brush still on the vanity. Not the perfectly folded gown across the bed. Not even the window, half-open like it was waiting for someone to come home.

I saw the feet first.

Pale. Dangling. Motionless.

No.

The chair was tipped over, resting on its side like it had fought to stop her. But it didn't. It couldn't.

Her hair swayed slightly from the draft, a golden curtain that barely brushed the floor. Her body, limp. Her dress, wrinkled like she hadn't cared how she looked.

Bethany.

My Bethany.

I dropped Kael's sword and his dagger. They clattered across the stone. My hands shook as I stumbled forward.

"No. No, no, no... what the fuck did you do?!"

I grabbed her ankles, held onto her cold, lifeless calves like it would anchor me in the storm crashing through my ribcage. Her head lolled a little with the motion, I noticed something in her hand.

Parchment.

Crushed and crinkled in her stiff fingers.

I had to pry them open. One by one. Her nails were purple, her skin like fucking ice, and I was crying... ugly, raw, guttural sobs that made my body convulse as I finally tore the note free.

I stared at it. Couldn't read it through the blur. I wiped my eyes on my blood-stained sleeve and held it up to the light...

I don't know who I'm writing this for.

I don't expect anyone to forgive me.

I betrayed the one person I would've walked through fire and brimstone barefooted for.

I thought I was protecting her. I thought I was doing the right thing.

But I was wrong.

I saw her. In the dungeon. I tried to speak to her. She wouldn't even look at me. And when she did... gods, the hatred in her eyes. It broke something in me.

I tried to fix it. I rode until my legs went numb. I found Kael. I led him and his men to the castle gates. I don't know if it worked. I don't know if she lived.

I came back here. To her bed. I laid there and cried until I couldn't breathe. And even if she did survive, I knew she'd never forgive me. I couldn't forgive myself.

They read the King's decree in the town square just as I tied off the rope.

And that's when I knew... I couldn't go on in a world where she looked at me like that.

Tell her... tell her I never stopped loving her and she will always be my one true friend.

I'm sorry I wasn't brave enough or strong enough...

Some sins don't get forgiven. Some just get buried.

-Bethany

I didn't remember screaming.

But I did.

A sound ripped from my throat that wasn't human. I tore the noose down and caught her as she fell into my arms, heavy and limp and wrong. Her neck was broken. Her skin was so cold.

"I wasn't done with you!" I howled, pressing my forehead to hers. "You don't get to fucking leave me too!"

I don't know how long I sat there, rocking her like a child, sobbing into her hair like she could still hear me.

Then I felt him.

The air shifted.

I looked up... and there he was.

Kael.

Leaning against the wall, arms crossed. Watching.

"Did you know?" I asked him.

He said nothing.

"Did she die for me? Is that what this is?"

Still nothing.

"FUCKING SAY SOMETHING!"

I threw a vase at him. It shattered against the wall.

But he was gone. Just a flicker. A hallucination. A ghost that wouldn't haunt me right.

I crumbled.

Dropped to my knees. Pulled Bethany's body back into my lap and wept until I had nothing left. Just an empty, goddamned husk of a woman who'd lost everything.

"You were supposed to stay with me..."

My whisper echoed in the silence like a curse.

And the room went quiet.

Just the sound of our breathing...

Mine still going.

Hers, long since stopped.

CHAPTER XLII

THE DEVIL IN THE GARDEN

ELYSANDRA

They found her at nightfall.

Curled up on the stone floor of her childhood chambers like a corpse that hadn't realized it was supposed to rot. Arms wrapped tight around Bethany's lifeless body, head buried in the stiffened, cold neck of the only person who ever dared call her "friend" without expecting a fucking crown in return.

Seraphina didn't look up when they entered. She didn't flinch when Alistair knelt beside her, or when the guards whispered amongst themselves about what to do. She just... murmured. A constant stream of broken thoughts and names: *Kael.. . Bethany... Kael... what did you do, Bethany... where are you, Kael... come back... I can't... I can't do this without you.*

It was a magnificent sight, truly.

I stood in the archway and watched her unravel, piece by precious piece. The girl had been forged in fire, then thrown back into the coals. And now here she was, shattered, grieving, drenched in her own silence. Broken. Utterly. Completely. And still somehow... standing in spirit.

Remarkable.

And that's when it hit me. That little prick in my gut. The extra soul I felt slip through the cracks during the siege. The one that didn't belong.

So, it was *her*.

I had wondered who it might be. *Prayed,* in my own twisted way, that it wasn't Bethany. And yet here we were. Death always knows how to make a fucking entrance.

When Seraphina finally snapped out of her daze, it wasn't with tears. It wasn't with some poetic monologue about love and loss.

It was a scream.

Raw. Animalistic. Her throat tore with it. Her eyes were bloodshot; her voice cracked with every syllable that followed.

"They burn tomorrow," she spat. "A *king's* funeral. Both of them. Kael and Bethany. I don't give a fuck how many men it takes, how much wood, how many hours you work. It happens. *At dusk.*"

She looked every god in the heavens dead in the face as if daring them to argue.

"Take my kingdom. Take my sanity. But if you take my grief and call it divine justice, I'll burn your fucking temples down myself."

And I... may have smiled.

It was just the right time to be *useful*.

When the others cleared the room, Alistair dragging the guards out by sheer tension in his jaw... I approached. Alone. Quiet.

She didn't speak.

Good. I wasn't here for permission.

"You're not wrong, you know," I whispered, standing beside the bed where Bethany had once curled up like a child afraid of the dark. "The gods do like to fuck with us. They play their little games. Move us like pieces on a board."

Still no answer. But her jaw clenched. Progress.

"Kael wasn't meant to die, not yet. And Bethany... she was never supposed to be the one who broke. They cheated. Changed the script."

I bent down and touched the cold floor. A shadow curled around my fingers like smoke. "But there's a loophole in every divine plan."

That made her look up. Her eyes were hollow, feral, bloodshot beyond recognition.

"If I wanted to see him again..." she rasped. "Could you...?"

I smiled, slow and serpentine.

"If you wanted to? My darling queen, I could *make it happen*. All it would take... is a deal."

Her hands twitched around Bethany's braid. Her breath hitched. Her soul cracked just wide enough for me to slip through.

"The gods don't deserve to write your story. You do. Let's make them choke on it. Let's make them *watch*."

I leaned closer, lips by her ear, my voice a lullaby dipped in arsenic.

"Let's make a deal."

SERAPHINA

"No."

It wasn't my voice.

Kael stood behind her. Behind Elysandra. Just out of reach.

No one else saw him.

Of course they didn't.

But I did.

His face was the same as the last time I saw it... blood-stained, defiant, beautiful. His sword had cut through kingdoms and kissed my skin with the weight of every promise he'd ever made. And now here he was. My ghost. My *king*.

I looked up into Elysandra's eyes. She was all charm and venom. She could make the stars kneel if she wanted to. I *wanted* to say yes.

I *needed* to say yes.

But Kael shook his head.

"Don't," he said. "Don't let her turn your grief into a leash."

I looked at him. At nothing. To everyone else, I probably looked fucking mad. Hell, maybe I *was*.

But I trusted him more dead than I'd ever trusted the living.

"She helped raise me," Kael whispered. "She's been watching all along. But her deals? They come wrapped in silk and lined with teeth."

I couldn't breathe. My throat burned. My arms still held Bethany like if I let go, the world would end.

"I just want you back," I whispered.

Kael stepped closer. "I never left. But you... if you take this deal, you'll lose yourself."

I looked back at Elysandra. Her face was a mask of intrigue and pretend sympathy. She was good. Too good.

"I'll keep that in mind," I said, barely audible.

She stood. Straightened her cloak. Her grin was pure wickedness.

"Well then," she said. "If you ever change your mind... the offer remains. All you need to do... is say so."

And then she was gone.

But Kael wasn't.

Not yet.

And neither was the storm brewing in my goddamn heart.

CHAPTER XLIII

ASHES TO ASHES

SERAPHINA

T he twin pyres stood tall on the blackened shores of Eldoria's great river... one for a king, one for a traitor who died with loyalty in her heart. The wind howled like it knew who we were burying. Or maybe it was Kael, still not ready to let go.

The sky above had the decency to mourn with us, covered in storm-gray clouds that dripped cold rain like tears from gods who'd watched this entire kingdom burn.

Kael's body was draped in the war banner of Morvath... dark, tattered, soaked in his blood. His sword rested on his chest, the dagger at his side. The blade that had started the war now would be buried with the man who tried to end it.

Bethany lay in white. I'd dressed her myself, the same gown she once wore at my coronation as princess. She looked peaceful, even though she'd died a storm of guilt and sorrow. I placed the parchment she'd written beside her, tucked between her fingers, like she could hold her apology into the next world.

The people had gathered. Soldiers. Civilians. Survivors. None spoke.

Not even Alistair, who stood at my side, silent for once, understanding that this moment didn't belong to words... it belonged to memory.

I stepped forward, slow, deliberate. Kael first.

"I never got a proper goodbye," I whispered, only loud enough for him.

I knelt beside him, fingers trailing across the edge of his jaw. He still looked like him. Fierce. Stubborn. Mine.

"You told me once that fire would be our ending," I said. "But maybe it's also the beginning."

I lit the torch.

And when I placed it at the base of his pyre, the flames roared to life like they recognized the man they were consuming.

Bethany was next.

I didn't speak at first. Just knelt. Took her hand.

"I hated you," I said. "But I also... I loved you."

I swallowed, jaw trembling.

"You should've told me. You should've stayed. You should've let me forgive you."

The torch slipped from my hand.

The fire took her too.

Two fires. One sky. And a hundred hearts breaking at once.

I stood between them as they burned. Watching. Waiting. Feeling.

When the smoke began to climb, curling toward the heavens like an offering, I placed a hand on my stomach.

Alistair noticed. His eyes flicked to my belly, then up to meet mine. His expression shifted.

"His," I said softly. "Kael's."

He said nothing. Just nodded once. That was enough.

I turned to the crowd.

"Let it be known," I called out, voice clear, unwavering despite the wind, "that today we bury a king and a fallen soul, both of whom died not for conquest... but for me."

Whispers.

I raised my hand.

"From this day forward, the Kingdoms of Eldoria and Morvath are no longer enemies. They are one. One banner. One people. One future. We move forward as Eldoria, unified and reborn."

They listened. Not a soul dared interrupt.

I wasn't finished.

"A bounty of 10,000 gold will be paid to the one who delivers Malakar... dead or alive. He is to be executed or arrested on sight. He will answer for every innocent life taken in this war."

And then, I turned my back on them.

Because I had one more goodbye left to give.

The fire was dying down now. Smoke curling like ink into the sky.

And there he was.

Kael.

Not in the flames... but standing beside them.

Clear as day.

No blood. No armor. Just him.

He smiled. Gods, that smile.

"Looks like you did it," he said, voice low, warm, devastating. "Burned it all down."

"I did," I whispered, tears slipping free.

"You saved them."

"I saved what was left."

He nodded.

We stared at each other, time holding its breath.

"I'm scared," I admitted. "Of what comes next. Of doing this alone."

"You're not alone," he said, taking a step closer. "You've got the fire now."

I reached for him.

But there was nothing to touch.

"Will I ever see you again?"

"Every time you look at our child."

My knees buckled, but I held myself upright.

"I don't want you to go."

"I'm not really gone, Seraphina. You carry me."

He turned then, walking into the smoke.

"Wait," I called.

He paused.

"I love you."

He looked back. That fucking smile again.

"I know."

And then he was gone.

The pyres burned down to ash.

And I walked away from them... not a queen, not a widow.

But something new.

Something forged in blood, and loss, and love.

Something unbreakable.

Seraphina

EPILOGUE
WHERE WEAVERS WEEP

ELYSANDRA

F ate is a cruel, elegant bitch.

She twists. She coils. She offers the illusion of free will, of triumph, of choice... then laughs from her throne when all paths lead right back to where she decreed them. And mortals? They dance for her. They think they are the ones who carve destiny into stone, but the blade is always in someone else's hand. Usually, mine.

I've watched kingdoms rise and burn into ash. I've watched lovers bleed and queens fall on their own swords. I've listened to prayers shouted at stars that no longer shine.

But once in a rare age... something else is born from the fire.

Something *new*.

Her name is **Vale**.

A fitting name, I thought, when I first saw her. Seraphina had gone into labor beneath the first blood moon since the unification. The screams echoed through the halls of the royal infirmary like a banshee mourning her own death. And then... silence. That haunting, heavy silence that only a mother's fear could conjure.

But then... she cried. Loud. Angry. Alive.

She had *his* eyes.

Kael's blue. That storm-washed sky, clear and cold. And her hair... snow white. Not the pale blonde of a noble house, no... *white*, like untouched frost clinging to ash. She was beautiful. She was fire-born. She was fated.

I remember Seraphina holding her close, her lips cracked and chapped, whispering prayers not to the gods, but to the dead. To Kael. To Bethany. To whoever might be listening, because the gods, as we both knew, were bastards.

They named her Vale. After the mountain pass where Kael once held the line, after the valley where the flames had licked the sky, after the silence that followed everything that had been lost.

But Seraphina was not naïve.

She knew.

Malakar had not been seen since the fall. No body. No blood. No bones. Just absence. That kind of silence is not peace. It is a promise waiting to be fulfilled.

So, Seraphina made a decision I did not see coming. She and Alistair found a farmer and his wife... a kind, infertile couple who had given up on their own miracle long ago. They lived on the edge of the northern ridge, far from court, far from whispers.

They were told only this: *Keep her safe. Keep her hidden. Never let her know who she is.*

And so, Vale became no one. No title. No throne. Just a little girl with curious eyes and an old soul.

But you and I both know the truth.

She is not no one.

She is the daughter of Kael of Morvath and Seraphina of Eldoria. She is born of ash and crowned in flame.

I have seen her birth a thousand times. In dreams. In visions. In the shiver of wind through bone trees beneath moons that no longer exist. The shape always shifts—sometimes Seraphina dies in labor. Sometimes the babe is stolen by cultists. Sometimes the world ends before she takes her first breath.

But in this timeline... she lives.

And I watch her.

Always from the shadows, of course. She does not know me. She must *not* know me...yet. But I see her chasing fireflies through the wheat. I watch her fall and skin her knees, then scowl at the sky like she's ready to punch the gods for daring to make her bleed. I see her pet stray animals and give them ridiculous names. She is *so* much like her father. And far more like her mother than anyone realizes.

She has already asked, more than once... if she can go into the forest. *My* forest. She calls it the Witchwood. The locals tell her stories, and she eats them up like sugar on her tongue. She is drawn to it, to me, though she does not know why.

She will.

One day, when the age is right, when Seraphina deems the kingdom stable enough to allow her daughter to train with the Knights of Luminara... when she believes the world is safe again... Vale will step forward into the light.

And then... the real war begins.

You see, the gods haven't left us. They're just *waiting*. Watching.

They've forged one queen.

They've taken one king.

They want more.

But they forgot one simple truth.

I'm still here.

And I've kept my promises. To Kael. To Seraphina. Even to Bethany, who still haunts me in ways I refuse to name.

The child is growing. Strong. Fierce. Reckless. Fate sings in her veins, and every time I see those piercing blue eyes... Kael's eyes, I remember that love, though fleeting, leaves scars that never fade.

Seraphina should be proud of her. And I think she is, in her own broken way. She still rules, yes, but her soul is buried beneath two pyres.

Still, her flame burns. And so does Vale's.

And I? I watch. I wait. I weave.

Because fate doesn't rest.

And neither do I.

There is always another reckoning...

Afterword
Beyond the Ash

If you made it here, you're the kind of reader I write for, the ones who aren't afraid to bleed a little just to feel something real.

I'm not gonna lie to you: parts of *Under Moonlit Ashes* broke me wide open while I wrote them. There are scenes in these pages where I cried like a damn fool at my own keyboard. Not because I didn't see it coming, but because I *felt* every damn thread snapping, same as you did.

This book is its own curse. It'll make you laugh in the dark, grieve for things you never had, and maybe mourn parts of yourself you didn't know were still alive. It's a perfect storm, a twisted carnival of heartbreak, hope, betrayal, and moments that'll stick under your skin long after you close the cover.

I hope you loved my characters, because they're yours now too. Kael, Seraphina, Elysandra, Bethany.... and yes Nibbles...*fucking* Nibbles; every one of them means something different to everyone who finds them. That's how it's supposed to be. What you see in them says as much about *you* as it does about me.

If you think you caught every secret this story is hiding, think again. There are hidden veins running through these pages... meanings I buried on purpose, truths that only show themselves to the ones willing to dig. You won't catch them all on your first read. Hell, you might not catch them all on your fifth. But they're there, waiting for the eyes sharp enough to see what's lurking in the ash.

I don't write books that vanish when you're done. I write ones that haunt and... now it's yours to carry.

Thank you for surviving it with me. Stay hungry. Stay haunted. Stay sharp. There's more coming... I promise you that.

-T.A. Thornwell

ABOUT THE AUTHOR

T.A. THORNWELL

T.A. Thornwell was born in the hidden hollers of Bluefield, West Virginia; a place where secrets fester in the dark and stories run thicker than the coal seams underfoot. He grew up on bitter coffee, busted knuckles, and the kind of truths you only whisper when the mountains can't hear.

Before turning pages into battlegrounds, **T.A. Thornwell** was chasing ink in a different form. As a young man, he landed his dream gig as an independent comic book artist, carving out panels and characters for small-press projects that have long since slipped into the shadows of out-of-print nostalgia.

When the comics faded, he traded the studio light for a welding hood and the black veins of Appalachian coal. 3 years of working underground and countless years working on the surface in the blue-collar grind forged a storyteller who understands grit in his bones... the kind of grit that shows up in every line he writes. Now he brings that same rough-edged work ethic to the page, welding words into kingdoms and carving out characters that hit just as hard as a steel beam under flame.

He writes because silence never suited him. He draws because sometimes the words bite too deep. And when he needs to shut the world up, he loses himself in video games, one more battlefield where the monsters make sense and the stakes feel honest. *(COD "Zombies Player", Ark: Survival Evolved and Ark: Survival Ascended, Elder Scrolls 5: Skyrim, and Elden Ring)*

Thornwell doesn't craft happy endings. He forges scars into scripture, kingdoms that fall, witches who scheme, lovers who bleed just to taste something real. Every page is a confession you can't wash off.

His greatest spark, though, is blood and bone... his daughter, **Katherine Andy**, a writer in her own right. She's shaping her debut novel now, a contemporary fantasy romance meant to burn its way through YA and NA hearts the same way her father's stories gut the rest.

These days, you'll find Thornwell somewhere between the pines... boots caked in mud, sketchbook smudged with ghosts, always chasing the next story that won't stay buried.

T.A. THORNWELL

Read him if you dare. Survive him if you can. But once you read Thornwell's words... you carry them forever.

OTHER BOOKS
BY T.A. THORNWELL

Eldoria: Forgotten Realm

Step into the dark heart of Eldoria, where old kingdoms crumble and dangerous magic stirs beneath the surface. You'll find some familiar faces; the shadows of characters you just met... and the fragile beginnings of Vale's story, a legacy that could change everything.

This is the first book in Thornwell's YA Fantasy series, packed with betrayal, power struggles, Sapphic closed-door romance and the kind of secrets that haunt bloodlines for generations.

Available now on Amazon in **Ebook ($4.99)**, **Paperback ($19.99)**, and **Hardcover ($29.99)**.

*Kindle Unlimited subscribers read for **FREE**.*

Eldoria: The Moonspire

The story doesn't end in the Forgotten Realm. Vale's journey deepens in *The Moonspire*. Old faces return, new allies emerge, and secrets long buried rise with a vengeance. The legendary Moonspire Circle; thought lost to time... resurfaces, its ancient magic stirring just as a new darkness creeps into Eldoria's veins.

At the heart of it all stands Elara... beloved and bound to a destiny far bigger than she ever imagined. To stand against what's coming, she must embrace a role she never wanted and unlock power that could save or shatter everything.

This is Book 2 in Thornwell's YA Fantasy series; where trust cuts like a knife, loyalty is tested in shadows, and hope is the sharpest weapon left.

Available now on Amazon in **Ebook ($4.99)** and **Paperback ($14.99)**.

*Kindle Unlimited subscribers read for **FREE**.*

www.ingramcontent.com/pod-product-compliance
Lightning Source LLC
Chambersburg PA
CBHW021957130726
47903CB00014B/1563